AJ pressed some dog treats into her hand.

He taught Lucie how to command Jetson to roll over, and as they all laughed at the dog's antics, she could see with her own eyes how Jetson's presence eased the mood. If only he could ease hers.

Something was niggling at her. The look on AJ's face when he'd suggested she must've had a boyfriend over the years. That *one* look had told her the thought affected him somehow.

Not that it should matter. It was definitely best to keep this professional and not spend any more time with him than necessary, she decided, listening to him explain to an elderly patient how Josiah and Ruby made homemade dog treats—he really was father of the year. Damn him for turning out so perfect.

Every time AJ caught her eyes, he looked away quickly, as if he'd been caught doing something illicit. It made her blood race. Maybe she wasn't imagining it now. Maybe there was something there.

No… Stop doing this to yourself, Lucie!

She had to stop telling herself that she and Austin Johnstone could ever be anything more than friends.

Dear Reader,

As a cockapoo mama myself I know how ~~needy and expensive~~ charming and intelligent our four-legged pals can be. But imagine if your pet could detect diseases as well, like the ones in our hero's training program.

There's lots of incredible work being done around canine assistance and the various roles dogs can play in the medical world. I was fascinated to learn more about it while writing this, and while watching our couple fall in love with each other as much as the dogs.

I hope your tails wag over this story, readers. Now go get loved up!

Becky x

FINDING FOREVER
WITH THE SINGLE DAD

———

BECKY WICKS

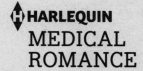

HARLEQUIN

MEDICAL
ROMANCE

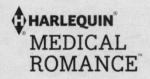

HARLEQUIN®
MEDICAL
ROMANCE™

Recycling programs
for this product may
not exist in your area.

ISBN-13: 978-1-335-59493-8

Finding Forever with the Single Dad

Copyright © 2023 by Becky Wicks

All rights reserved. No part of this book may be used or reproduced in
any manner whatsoever without written permission except in the case of
brief quotations embodied in critical articles and reviews.

This is a work of fiction. Names, characters, places and incidents
are either the product of the author's imagination or are used fictitiously.
Any resemblance to actual persons, living or dead, businesses,
companies, events or locales is entirely coincidental.

For questions and comments about the quality of this book,
please contact us at CustomerService@Harlequin.com.

Harlequin Enterprises ULC
22 Adelaide St. West, 41st Floor
Toronto, Ontario M5H 4E3, Canada
www.Harlequin.com

Printed in U.S.A.

Born in the UK, **Becky Wicks** has suffered interminable wanderlust from an early age. She's lived and worked all over the world, from London to Dubai, Sydney, Bali, NYC and Amsterdam. She's written for the likes of *GQ*, *Hello!*, *Fabulous* and *Time Out*, a host of YA romance, plus three travel memoirs—*Burqalicious*, *Balilicious* and *Latinalicious* (HarperCollins, Australia). Now she blends travel with romance for Harlequin and loves every minute! Tweet her @bex_wicks and subscribe at beckywicks.com.

Books by Becky Wicks

Harlequin Medical Romance

Visit the Author Profile page at Harlequin.com.

CHAPTER ONE

'LUCIE HENDERSON? Is that really you?'

Lucie's feet found their way to the chocolate shop doorway. Gramma May's good friend Cynthia hugged her warmly to her bosom. 'Oh, my goodness, duck…it's been so long. I thought you were off saving the world! What brings you back to Yorkshire?'

'Oh, you know…' Lucie shrugged.

If she told Cynthia she was here not only to fill a temporary role at the Brookborough general practice, but to recuperate after a tragedy that had plagued her dreams ever since it had happened, she might as well announce it on a megaphone to the entire village. Brookborough was the place where secrecy came to die. Everyone knew everyone else's business on this side of the North Yorkshire Moors. The last thing she needed was for people to start looking at her in sympathy.

'Tell me what I've missed, Cynthia. When did I last see you? I think I was eighteen…'

Soon, the fragrant chocolate shop had her

trapped in its cosy interior. She sampled white bon-bons and cinnamon swirls while Cynthia shared the highlights of what she'd missed. The cannon fire of questions she fired wasn't so easy to swallow.

'What was it like, working in Nepal?'
'How are things there now, after the tragedy?'
'How are you, really?'

Lucie was polite, but the barrage of questions was enough to shake her back into a state she hadn't been in since the earthquake. She was so far away from where she was needed…

Cynthia had that look in her eyes now. Narrowed, pensive, a little scared that she might hear or say something that made them both feel uncomfortable. Obviously Gramma May must have told her oldest friend a few things about her specialism in mental health, her international placements with the Medicine Relief Operatives out in distant disaster zones, but how much did anyone know about what had happened to her colleague Jorge that day at the school on the mountain road in Nepal?

'Wow, this is good,' she heard herself say.

The chocolate was demanding full custody of her attention now, forcing her to acknowledge the taste of her childhood. She might as well have taken a bite of Austin Johnstone too, she thought. This used to be their number one Saturday morning activity.

It wasn't hard to recall standing with her best friend on the steps of the Grade Two listed All Saints' Church on the night of the Scarecrow Festival. Austin Johnstone—better known as AJ to everyone around here—would always buy her one chocolate and dare her to make it last all day. She could never do it. The chocolates were just too good.

'Just made 'em this morning, pet.' Cynthia rustled a paper bag and popped more chocolates into it. 'Take a couple home for May, why don't you? Bert used to buy her these, and I know she loves them.'

I won't eat it, I won't eat it...not like AJ would have done.

The scent of the sweet chocolate gift for Gramma, in honour of Lucie's late Grampa Bert, tempted her from her handbag as she walked on.

Stopping at the bottom of the hill, she saw All Saints' Church peering down at her like a weathered, wise brown owl. Her gaze ran over the gravestones protruding from the grassy knoll where AJ had once set up a séance. He'd planned for them to reach the spirit of the Black Knight of the North, who supposedly rested there. They'd done all kinds of stupid things in those days, them and their friends, making their own entertainment in a place the size of a postage stamp.

Until AJ had ruined everything, by hooking up with Claire Bainbridge.

Lucie scowled as she walked on. Of course he'd charge into her brain like that pushy Black Knight. Even the streams that flowed alongside the honey-coloured stone cottages with their picture-postcard pantile roofs couldn't force the memories away. Thank goodness their paths wouldn't cross while she was here.

Gramma May had told her that he'd moved to London. She'd said nothing else—just that he'd moved there and was a very well-respected psychiatrist. Lucie had made the mistake of asking about him years ago and had discovered he'd got married and had two kids. Twins, no less. That had *not* been a good day. Whenever she'd thought about looking him up online after that she'd chickened out. She knew she'd only find photos of him and Claire, all happily married, nesting with their beautiful twin babies.

Nope. No, thanks.

So, the blond-haired, blue-eyed former Mr Popularity was a psychiatrist. It made sense. He always had been the caring kind. Well, until he'd hooked up with Claire, she thought, wrinkling up her nose.

She'd never forgotten the bone-deep hurt and mortification she'd felt that night she'd stood outside his bedroom door, listening to him in there, laughing with Claire about her! Claire had been teasing him for the way 'little lost Lucie' always followed him around like a puppy dog, and he'd said nothing. Absolutely nothing to defend Lucie, who was supposed to be his best friend.

It didn't seem to matter how many time zones and disaster areas she'd found herself in since— she could still be back there in a flash. Eighteen years old, secretly, hopelessly in love with the most popular guy in Brookborough, and listening to Claire telling him, *'Lucie is seriously cramping your style, AJ. How about you let me show you some things little lost Lucie never could?'*

The devastation. The total humiliation of hearing him betray their friendship like that. She'd fallen for him hard. He'd been her rock since he'd found her crying, back when she'd been nine and the new girl in town. Everyone had been whispering about her at school, calling her 'the American orphan'. He'd stood up for her—a real-life hero. She'd barely been able to find the words to tell him about the fire on a campsite that had killed her parents while she'd been watching illicit horror films with her babysitter in Denver. Or her busy, travel-obsessed Aunt Lina, who'd taken her in for a while, but who ultimately hadn't much wanted to be tied down with a grieving child, and had consequently flown her from Colorado to the UK, to be raised by her paternal grandparents instead.

AJ had always been there for her—as a friend, nothing more. He hadn't left her side for a month after Grampa Bert's death. She'd been fourteen then. He hadn't agreed when she'd told him it was her fault. But of course it was her fault. Grampa had been forced to go back to work after she'd arrived, instead of retiring as he'd planned, so they could afford to look after her. He'd worked so hard he'd had a heart attack and died way too young.

'Lucie? Lucie Henderson?'

Flora McNally bustled out onto the street from the gift shop, all smiles.

'Hi, Flora, you look well.'

'What a lovely surprise! May did say you were coming home for a while. How long do we have you for, Little Lu?'

Little Lu. Wow… No one had called her that when she was standing on stages, establishing civic engagement alliances, advocating for reducing disaster risks… It would have made her smile if it hadn't reminded her of Claire's snide comments all over again.

White-haired Flora had crossed her arms. Lucie smoothed her fringe, shook her hair behind her shoulders. Did her thirty-four-year-old self appear so very different from the teenager with a pixie cut who'd switched this place for America?

'I'll be here a couple of months, give or take.'

'May's so very proud of you, pet,' Flora cooed, and her eyes shone with the same look Lucie had seen on Cynthia's face in the chocolate shop. 'What you must have gone through… It was all over the news. I heard you pulled some kids out of the rubble in Nepal? You're lucky to be alive... well done, you.'

Lucie thanked her, eyeing the ground. It didn't take much to make the memories come raging back. The school walls collapsing on Jorge. The creaking cascade of concrete and steel. The water tank toppling from its perch... They'd said it was a thousand gallons. She'd pulled the others out—the three kids had *had* to come first—as soon as the rumble had begun. Brie and Jero from her team had followed after, cut up and bloodied, but fine. They'd called it a miracle that she'd got out uninjured, but she hadn't been able to save Jorge.

They'd given her a medal after that. She'd felt like a total fake, accepting it.

Lucie edged along the pathway as Flora talked. How many more people was she failing just by being *here*? Sure, she had nightmares about Nepal sometimes—but it was nothing really. Not when there were still people out there she could be helping with Medicine Relief Operatives. This hiatus was going to be good for her—a nice, cosy locum GP position to take her mind off things for a bit, and a chance to spend more time with Gramma May. But the sooner she could get back out there, where she belonged, the better.

'Are you OK, pet? You've gone a bit pale.' Flora caught her arm.

'I'm fine. I have to be on my way, but it's nice to see you, Flora.'

Hitting a left at the pub, she took the path along the stream back to Gramma's. It seemed as good a path as any, going past the storybook Beck Isle Cottage. The gentle sound of the babbling water was always better than any CD.

This had always been her favourite part of the village and today every lungful of cool early-March air was a balm. AJ had kissed her here, aged ten and a bit, on the little bridge that boasted a world-famous chocolate-box view. If her memories were correct, she'd dared him to do it a couple of weeks after a dance in the school gym. He'd bought her a chocolate bar that night. She'd thought at the time that his gift had meant something. Clearly, it hadn't.

The way he'd swiped at his mouth afterwards, as if kissing a girl was the equivalent of eating cat food, had not done wonders for her self-esteem. Neither had seeing him with a steady stream of girls after that, while *she* had remained firmly in the friend zone. *Ugh.*

She'd never expected Claire, though. She'd high-tailed it back down his stairs and out through the door as fast as a lightning bolt after hearing them together in his room, before she'd been forced to hear anything worse. As if the only reason she'd run to him in the first place hadn't been bad enough… She'd just heard Gramma May admit to Cynthia that she and Grampa Bert had always wanted to travel in their retirement, and that Lucie had stopped them!

Well, not in those words exactly. She knew her grandparents loved her. But she was the reason they hadn't been able to travel as they'd planned before Grampa died.

Cynthia had said that maybe May could travel alone, without Grampa, once Lucie had gone away to university. But May had replied that she probably would not. She would wait, because Lucie would be home frequently for holidays.

She had concluded from that that she was *still* stopping Gramma from living the life she'd wanted before they'd been forced to take her in!

She'd wanted to tell AJ how Aunt Lina had emailed her, offering to pay for her medical training if she agreed to go back to the US and get to know her and her American roots. Apparently, Lina felt pretty bad for being too young and busy and grieving to keep her in America after her sister's death.

She'd hoped that maybe AJ would say she didn't have to go, and that after nine years her home was there. That had been her hope. But after hearing what she'd heard—first Gramma and Cynthia's conversation, and then AJ and Claire's—she'd run home, opened her laptop and taken her aunt up on the offer instead, chasing her dream of becoming a doctor.

She'd never even said goodbye to AJ. He probably hadn't missed her always following him around like a puppy dog, cramping his style, anyway.

Lucie took the little path along the stream, breathing in the spring scent of the trees. She was still failing to shove the memories of AJ from her head when something huge, dark and furry seemed to launch at her from nowhere.

She shrieked, just as a man's panicked warning was hollered at her from a distance.

What the…?

Before she could gather her thoughts, her feet were scrambling for solid ground. The man sprinted towards her, still yelling.

Too late.

Lucie lost her balance and toppled off the grassy bank straight into the icy stream.

CHAPTER TWO

LUCIE WAS MORE mortified than cold, flailing like an octopus in the water, her feet struggling for a grip on the mossy bottom. No sooner had she managed to sort of half-stand, her hair slapped in sodden streaks to her face, than a broad-shouldered man came into view, wading towards her.

'Here, take my hand!'

Lucie blinked, trying to bring him into focus. Leaves and twigs were twirling around her ankles in a frozen serenade. The icy water sloshed at the bank, where a dark brown Labrador paced the path, barking an alert. So *that* was what had forced her into the water!

'I've got you!' The man was behind her now. He looped his arms under her shoulders, bringing her to a fully standing position. 'You're OK!'

She slumped against him, catching her breath. Her red-heeled boots were stuck between stones and fallen branches—her poor boots...they'd take *weeks* to dry.

'Wrong kind of shoes for fly fishing, I see,' he said. 'Hold still.'

That voice.

Her stomach shot to her throat, just as she found herself lifted fully into the man's arms. Five feet in the air, with water pouring from the tops of her boots, she found there were no words to say as two familiar almond-shaped eyes met hers close up, and then grew so wide she thought he was going to drop her straight back into the water.

Here he was. Austin Johnstone. *AJ.* Thick caramel-blond hair, blue-grey eyes that could undo you…holding her up in a stream.

'Lucie?'

She blinked, aghast, feeling butterflies going bonkers in her stomach, then made to break free. He held her even tighter against his impressively muscular chest.

'Put me down!'

Really?

Trust the man who'd waded in after her to be AJ, of all the people in this town. She flailed her arms against him in a pathetic twisty motion, trying to break free of him, but he held tighter still, as if she was nothing but a bag of weightless balloons that might just float away.

'I said put me down, AJ!'

'OK… OK.'

A look of something like annoyance pushed all amusement from his face. He strode with her back to the bank, where he deposited her carefully onto the grass.

'It's nice to see you, too, Lucie,' he said dryly, as his hair flopped damply over his forehead. 'There's a leaf in your hair, by the way.'

She growled and tore off her waterlogged jacket, wringing it out. AJ stepped up beside her as she swiped at her hair, sending the leaf into the air, before all six feet of him straightened before her, commanding her full attention. His hard chest... those broad shoulders that had supported her head for so many train and bus rides...the trace of a beard he'd definitely never had before. He looked good with a beard, actually. Very good. Better looking than ever.

But of course he would be.

Her boots were *destroyed*.

'What are you doing here?' she spluttered.

'I could ask you the same thing.'

Her cheeks flamed hot—an old giveaway. She looked away, so her eyes wouldn't doubly betray her and reveal the burning fire in her belly.

He'd taken his shoes off. His maroon sweater was only wet around the chest and arms, but he pulled it off anyway, revealing a white T-shirt that clung to his washboard muscles. She did a double take as he offered his jumper to her, but no way was she accepting.

'Just take it,' he implored, holding it out.

'I'm fine,' she said tightly, resisting the urge to

grab it and smell it. He'd always used to smell so good. His clothes had fallen off her slim frame, but she'd still borrowed his T-shirts all the time anyway. 'I'm heading to Gramma's.'

The Labrador had finally ceased its barking. It lay panting in a patch of leaves on the grass under the trees, as if butter wouldn't melt.

'You need to control your dog,' she scolded. 'Does it always throw innocent people into streams?'

She'd said it mostly to fill the awkward silence while her mind spun. This might have been the right moment to storm away with what was left of her dignity, but somehow her feet refused to move—and not just because her poor boots were still sloshing. What was he doing here, anyway? Visiting family and friends with Claire and the kids?

Ugh... She didn't even want to know.

'Jetson doesn't usually do this,' AJ told her apologetically, pushing the thick mop of hair from his forehead.

It was darker than she remembered.

Antagonised, she huffed. 'Well, he's done it now! Since when do you like dogs, anyway?'

'I always liked dogs. I just never had one till I started working with them.'

Working with them? Wasn't he a psychiatrist?

'Anyway...' He bit back a laugh, no doubt at the

look on her face. 'It's bizarre, honestly. He never does that—do you, buddy?'

The dog laid its head on its paws and heaved a sigh. Lucie stared at it warily. Maybe the dog had sensed a connection between them—some lingering, thinning thread that used to tie their two souls together. Dogs were clever. Weird, but clever.

No. She was *annoyed*. Not *amused*. There was no chance she was smiling at him or his goofy dog, now or ever. Not after he'd failed to defend her, and their friendship, to Claire. It had cut her to the quick.

God, would you listen to yourself? That was years ago. You need to let it go.

AJ was still grinning at her. His familiar eyes traced along her body while water trickled down her back into her underwear. Why was he looking at her like that?

'I have to go,' she announced weakly, finally getting her feet to move in the opposite direction, back towards the main road. It was all she could do not to waddle like a deformed penguin.

'Lucie?'

She paused. His voice behind her held the gut-twisting tone of the boy she'd worshipped since the age of nine, plus some small hint of a plea that should have been satisfying after all this time, but only seemed to twist the key in a door she'd firmly bolted shut.

Her heart was back to racing like a freight train.

'What?'

'Will you let me make this up to you?'

Scraping back her bedraggled hair, she turned again, clocking the bulging biceps as he fished for sunglasses in his pockets. Even soaking wet, he was delicious. Why couldn't the sight of him repulse her? Instead it was igniting a million memories, all of them from before the time she'd heard solid proof of her love for him being unrequited, loud and clear through his bedroom door.

Not that he knew she'd heard anything—even though they were always walking in and out of each other's houses back then.

'Dinner tonight?' He slid his feet back into his shoes, which somehow he managed to make look sexy. 'I'll pick you up.'

She scanned his blue-grey eyes. Dammit, he was looking hotter with every passing second. All grown up. A man now, not a teenager.

'How do you know where I'm staying?'

He stared her down. 'You literally just said you were going to May's.'

Lucie frowned. This was all so strange...but so familiar at the same time. Maybe a part of her *did* want to know what he'd been up to the whole time she'd refused to accept him as a friend or follower on every single one of her social media accounts.

'Fine,' she heard herself saying. 'You *do* owe me, AJ.'

For a lot of things, she added silently.

'About that,' he said now, slinging his sweater over his shoulders like a model on a Yorkshire postcard. 'No one calls me AJ any more. It's Austin Johnstone.'

'Well, *I'm* back now,' she sniped, battling a fresh, unwelcome surge of longing. *God, he was hot.* 'And you'll always be AJ to me.'

A smile of something like admiration flickered in his eyes. She would not wait around for it to reach his mouth. Her heart was already in her throat and there was no way she was letting on how his presence was affecting her.

'Pick me up at seven,' she instructed, and turned on her soaking wet heels.

It was tough not to squelch as she made her undignified exit. And she felt his eyes burning into her back the whole way to the bridge.

CHAPTER THREE

'WHERE ARE YOU GOING, Dad?'

The twins cast their blue-eyed gazes up at him from their chairs. 'You smell nice,' Ruby observed.

'Out with an old friend,' he told them quickly, loading their dinner bowls haphazardly into the dishwasher.

'That's right…an old *friend*.'

Belle's voice was mocking, in the good-natured way his sister always spoke, as she left her chair, shooing him away from the dishwasher.

'You'd better go—you'll be late. I've got this.'

Jetson padded in from the lounge area, as if sensing that it was his turn now to help keep watch.

Josiah threw a plastic car in the direction of the blaring TV.

'Josiah, don't throw things at the TV. If you don't like what's on, turn it off. Jetson, fetch the toy.'

At Belle's instructions, Josiah marched to the TV while the dog went straight for the car. He placed the toy at his sister's feet.

'Nice work, sis!' Austin was impressed.

Belle was learning a few things about dogs from him, and as Chief Nursing Officer in the local nursing home she'd also been the hugest supporter of Thera Pups since he'd launched the company. She'd hooked him up with many regular visits to Lavender Springs.

Belle loved the people in that nursing home. Almost as much as everyone loved the dogs he sent there to keep them company twice a week. There was a lot to be said for animal-assisted intervention, and more benefits still to discover. Her championing him in every aspect of his life was something he could never be thankful enough for. And she was so good at distracting the twins when he held his online evening seminars, too.

There were many people he'd inspired to set up similar canine assistance companies all over the country. Especially since he'd started sharing the fact that his research—soon to be shared fully, in the paper he was writing—showed the potential for dogs to detect cancer in humans.

Jetson had already perfected the ability to detect impending migraines and low blood sugar in people and signal them to AJ. But they were still developing the disease detection training programme. More volunteers wanted to be involved all the time—which was the reason he was so damn busy now.

He hovered in the doorway and feigned a sigh that implied more concern about his sister's impending departure than he wanted to show. 'What will I do without you living here with us, Belle?'

'You'll be just fine.' She smiled warmly at him. 'It's been long enough, Austin. You're doing OK now. Ebby would be proud of you.'

A lump wedged in his throat. Sometimes he pictured Ebby, looking down on himself and the kids. Her tight, springy curls had used to bounce in a certain way when she shook her head in loving disapproval, and they'd be bouncing all the time now, if she saw the way he did things sometimes.

Over five years without her now. Over five years since Josiah and Ruby were born.

It *was* easier to smile these days, though. The days when he'd hardly been able to get out of bed and put the cornflake box on the table were behind him.

It had felt right at the time, selling their London place and buying the family home in Brookborough from Mum and Dad after they'd gone to live abroad for his mum's health. Ebby's life insurance, plus the money from the London house, had meant he didn't have to work for a while, and he'd been able to concentrate on making sure the twins were OK, while living in the place where people knew him best. Belle had done more than enough, too, moving in here with him, making herself a saint as well as a live-in nanny.

But now her engagement ring from Bryce sparkled like a diamond-encrusted ice cube on her fin-

ger. They'd all miss her when she moved to Leeds.
He'd been thinking of selling this house, too. Getting something smaller he could manage on his
own, as well as dealing with the mountain of work
he kept piling on himself.

'Why are you still standing there? Go!' Belle
told him, as she rooted in the freezer and tossed
choc ices to Ruby and Josiah.

They clawed at the wrappers like ravenous
birds, despite the stew he'd just served them.

Belle called out behind him. 'Give Lucie my
love, and tell her I want a date with her of my
own soon!'

'It's not a date,' he said, with one hand on the
door. 'She's just back visiting May. This is my attempt at being civil.'

As if Lucie would want a date with him. This
was the girl who'd left for America without even
saying goodbye to him, before blocking him from
any contact with her. It had been as if, after being
his friend all those years, she'd suddenly wanted
to erase him altogether from her world.

It had taken him months, maybe *years* to get
over that, seeing as he'd been tethered to her since
childhood. He never had understood what he'd
done to make her push him away like that.

Austin took the familiar road past the green and
its old stocks, where people had used to throw rotten fruit at miscreants. They'd been the miscreants
back then—him and Lucie. She'd been so much

his sidekick for all those years that he'd never been able to get up the courage to put everything on the line and tell her how he really felt about her.

It was probably a good thing, though. Clearly she'd never carried the same torch for him.

After she'd left, she'd still been everywhere he looked in this town. He hadn't been able to leave for university fast enough.

He knew practically nothing about her now, except that she'd won a bravery award for saving some children from a school after an earthquake in Nepal. Everyone here had talked about that for months. Why was she back in Brookborough now?

Earlier, when he'd realised it was her in that stream, he'd almost dropped her in shock. Even when she was angry, she was mesmerising. Once she'd been a lost little girl with an American accent. He'd often found her on the steps of Gramma May's house. She'd used to cry a lot. But then she'd grown up—fast.

There had been something indefinable about her that he'd never been able to pinpoint. A kind of inner fire…a defiance that had him itching to be around her, to hear her next plan or ambition. He'd never been able to keep up.

Then she'd left to study medicine in America without even telling him. He'd had to hear it from Gramma May. And Lucie had blocked him… ceased to need him. All on her terms.

Love. *Hate*. Love. *Hate*.

He'd felt both for her—equally fiercely. Which was why he was here tonight. Maybe he'd finally get some answers…

A familiar shadow drifted towards the door behind the glass. Gramma May answered the buzzer, nodded at him knowingly. 'She's upstairs. How are you doing, pet?'

'You know…'

He could tell his indifferent shrug didn't fool her. His neck prickled hot under his scarf as he looked over May's shoulder to the staircase.

'And how are Josiah and Ruby…?'

Austin barely heard her. Lucie had appeared from her old room on the landing. She glided down the staircase, finding his eyes from under a blunt ragdoll fringe. Her brown eyes were unreadable, but the hallway slipped away. This was definitely not the drenched unfortunate he'd pulled from the stream earlier. This was a grown-up Lucie. Still a force to be reckoned with, a beautiful tornado as always, sending him spinning.

His throat felt scratchy. 'You look nice.' He rubbed his neck as Gramma May spun around.

'Oh, you do. Where are you going on your date?'

'It's not a date,' they both chorused.

Lucie rolled her eyes at him, just like she used to. He half laughed at their secret code for *adults know nothing*. It lifted the tension a little.

'Well, you kids have fun now.'

May suppressed a smile. She had the same look on her face he'd just seen on Belle's—as if they were both plotting something. They knew he and Lucie had only ever been friends. But they also suspected he'd always had a crush on her—and knew that he hadn't dated anyone since Ebby died.

'Well, where are you taking me?'

Lucie slipped on a pair of flats as May closed the living room door behind her. The TV flickered through the glass door. They'd used to watch cartoons and make the cat climb homemade ladders made from cardboard boxes in there…and later he'd almost kissed her, but had chickened out. Again.

'The Old Ram Inn,' he responded.

Although she was a little overdressed for the sandstone corner pub. They'd used to meet there every Friday with the gang. Maybe he should've gone to more effort and booked the Thai place on the edge of town. But he'd got back late from his last appointment in Pickering.

'Ooh! The Old Ram Inn. Do they still have that steak and ale pie with those lovely big fat chips?'

'Of course.' He grinned. She looked like a kid again, asking that.

'And the old red carpet that looks like something from an eighties casino?'

'The one and only,' he confirmed.

Lucie nodded, as if checking off something from

a list she might've made on the plane here from…
Nepal?

'Good, I've missed it. Lead the way.'

He watched Lucie drumming her nails against the
salt shaker while they waited for their dinner. The
pub was as busy as ever. But despite the background noise of clanging cutlery and laughter, an
uncomfortable tension was drifting up between
them.

'So…' Austin started, searching his brain.

Lucie tossed her shiny hair over her shoulder
and fiddled with the collar on her blazer. 'So…'
she echoed, letting her gaze wander, as if she was
looking for an escape route already.

'You made the front page of the local paper.
Your heroic rescue and award. Everyone was talking about it. I would have congratulated you myself if you hadn't blocked me from every single
angle. There was no way for me to contact you.'

Lucie bristled.

His words had come out before he'd had time to
curb them, but she must have seen them coming.

Their pies arrived. Lucie stared at the steaming
plate of steak and ale as a bowl of chips was placed
between them. The waitress eyed them with interest as she poured the gravy. *Everyone* here was
looking at them. To those who didn't know Lucie
it must *look* as if he was on a date.

AJ squared his shoulders. Lucie jabbed her fork into a chip and twisted it.

'We're not going to talk about all that, are we?' she said finally, meeting his eyes.

The warning in her tone riled him up. 'Why did you block me, Lucie?'

She glared. 'I didn't think you'd even notice.'

'What? Why would you say that? You treated me like I tried to strangle you in the street or something! What did I do that was so wrong?'

Lucie huffed through her nose. 'It doesn't matter now, AJ. It was years ago. Is that why you brought me here? To dredge up the past?'

Austin sucked air through his nostrils till the vinegar on his chips burned his throat. Old Nigel— the Saturday market fruit and veg guy—was staring at them from the bar. Something about sitting opposite Lucie had him acting like a teenager again. He made an effort to calm down.

'We spent *all* our time together,' he hissed under his breath. 'Then you just…left. Without a word, Lucie. It just doesn't add up.'

'Why don't you ask Claire Bainbridge?'

Austin racked his brains, drawing a blank. What did Belle's friend Claire have to do with anything? 'I literally have *no* idea what you—'

'I told you…it doesn't matter now, does it?' she clipped, but the fire behind her eyes was raging.

For the life of him he couldn't imagine what she meant.

'Let's talk about you, *Austin Johnstone*. I hear you're married now, living in London. I guess you're here visiting your parents. How are they?'

Now it was his turn to clam up. Didn't she know? Hadn't Gramma May told her?

The way she was looking between him and her dinner told him that, no, she knew nothing.

'My wife passed away,' he said quietly. 'It's just me and the twins now. We moved back here from London a few years ago. I bought Mum and Dad's house when they moved to the Italian coast for Mum's asthma.'

Lucie's eyes grew round. She pushed her plate aside and reached across the table, almost sending the chips to the carpet, clasping his hands tightly. Her eyes flooded with horror and grief. It swept him up till he felt like a surfer trying to ride a tsunami.

'AJ… I'm so very sorry…poor Claire."
Claire?
He pulled his hands back. 'What is it with you and Claire? I wasn't married to Claire! Her name was Ebony—Ebby. We called her Ebby.'

Lucie's face was ghost-white. 'Ebby…?'

Austin's chest felt too small for his heavy heartbeat. 'Did May tell you nothing?'

'I told her not to,' she said in a small voice, tearing at a napkin. 'I wanted a clean break from Yorkshire, else I would have been too homesick. I wanted to focus on my studies. All I knew was that you practised psychiatry and had a wife and children…' She trailed off. 'But that's beside the point. I'm *so* sorry for your loss, AJ.'

His head reeled as she frowned in consternation, as if something else was just sinking in. 'Did you say you bought your parents' house?'

CHAPTER FOUR

LUCIE BATTLED WITH surging emotions that may have included something as annoying as envy as AJ described his son and daughter. Josiah was the loud one, the cheeky one, who always had something to say. Ruby was the quiet, thoughtful one. She cared deeply, beyond her five and a bit years, about everything and everyone. She adored her outspoken brother.

AJ was a besotted father. That much was apparent.

It wasn't hard to imagine what they looked like. They were probably beautiful. Maybe they had blue eyes and blond hair, like he'd used to have before he got this hot and toned and manly. Or maybe they looked like Ebby. Whoever Ebby was.

This was just...unreal. All this time she'd assumed he'd married Claire Bainbridge! Maybe that *was* a bit of a ridiculous assumption, now that she thought about it—they were only eighteen when she'd left—but her jealous imagination had filled in all the blanks while she'd blocked him, in case her stupid, desolate heart was forced to take another hit. Of course she wasn't about to admit how she'd came to make that assumption in the first place—sneaking in, eavesdropping, her heart thrumming with a puppy dog love he would never return… But here he was a widower, a single father.

Poor AJ.

'How did she die, if you don't mind me asking?' she dared.

The waitress took away their half-eaten pies.

It must've been something bad, and sudden.

She'd left young twins behind.

'She was out with friends,' he said finally. 'Her first night out since the babies were born. But she wanted to come home early—you know how new mothers are.'

Lucie murmured in sympathy. Though how would she know? The concept of motherhood, of an actual home, a family who needed and wanted her around, was alien to her. She'd lived out of a suitcase for years and loved it.

Most of the time.

'When she didn't come home, hours after she was meant to, I got worried, drove around looking for her. Then the police called. She hadn't even made it back to her car.'

He paused, twirled his pint glass between them, eyed her over it.

'The two lads who hit her in their Land Rover

had been drinking for thirteen hours straight. She died on the way to the hospital.'

Lucie's hands flew over her mouth. What the hell could she say to that, except reiterate how deeply sorry she was? Her apologies for his loss sounded hollow to her own ears. She'd never even met the woman, but she must have been something truly special if AJ had married her.

He told her some more about how he'd come back home, bought the family house after his parents had moved to Italy. This was the best place to bring up the twins, he said.

God, just the thought of losing a life partner... someone you'd built a new world with, made *children* with...how was he still standing?

Losing her parents had been a life-altering tragedy, but she'd been nine, almost too young for it to sink in at the time. It was the consequences she'd felt most, as the years had crept on without them. A sense of incompletion and inadequacy around those who *hadn't* been abandoned and sent away. A need to do things for herself, first and foremost, because people left, or died, and nothing lasted for ever.

'So, how long are you in town for?'

AJ took another swig of his drink. Obviously he wanted to change the subject—and who could blame him?

The wobble in her voice when she spoke made his eyebrows rise. 'I...um...took the locum position at the Brookborough Surgery. It's a two-month contract. I thought I'd take a break from Medicine Relief Operatives for a while…'

She tailed off. He was leaning closer now over the table, and his eyes were all-seeing. The boy who'd asked her so many times why she was crying had never pushed her. Instead he'd made her laugh, made her feel she hadn't quite lost *everything*.

'I have these dreams sometimes. Since the earthquake, you know? I watched a good friend die right in front of me. Yes, they gave me a medal for getting those children out, but I was the one who led Jorge into that school in the first place…'

'You led him in?'

'The earthquake happened after we'd stepped inside.'

She took a sip of wine. The sour taste scored her throat, while sympathy shone in his eyes. They had nothing in common—not where death was concerned. He had no idea how much she blamed herself for Jorge. First her Grampa Bert, then Jorge…

'Yes. Anyway, MRO offered me some time off between projects. Auntie Lina has moved to a condo in Miami, which isn't exactly peaceful, and I thought Gramma May could do with the company here. She's come out to America a couple of times to see me, in between projects, but it just seemed like a good time for me to come back to Brookborough.'

She crossed her legs uncomfortably. What on earth was making her tell AJ all this about herself?

The fact that you loved him once. And part of you always wished you were Claire...or, as it turns out, Ebby.

'So, you're still recuperating from trauma to some extent,' he said, thoughtfully.

His look shot her back to the time he'd homed in on her mouth in Gramma May's living room, when she'd been heavy with grief over Grampa Bert's passing. That one time when she'd seriously thought he might be about to kiss her of his own volition then didn't.

'I suppose we'll be seeing each other around,' he continued.

The pub chatter fell away as he searched her eyes.

No matter what had passed between them, what he'd endured without her knowing, there was something about him she'd never been able to forget. His absolute openness and honesty...his heart of gold. Whenever AJ looked at you, you felt like the only person in his universe.

It was exactly why the thing with Claire Bainbridge had shocked her so much. It had been just so *unlike* him to go for someone like her. Claire hadn't even been his type.

'You know what helped me with my dreams after Ebby died?' he said now.

She cocked her head. He'd had bad dreams, too?

Did he still have them? It would feel invasive, asking him any more questions now—like how they'd met, how he'd proposed, how he was coping alone, being a single dad with twins. Instead, she asked, 'What?'

'The dogs,' he answered. 'Remember Jamesy Abbot? The kid with ADD who used to jump out of the window in French class when Mrs De Ville wasn't looking and walk back in through the front door?'

She laughed at the memory. 'Our poor teacher... she was always so confused.'

'Right! Well, he asked me to look after his Golden Retriever, Star Lord, a couple of years after Ebby died. His therapy dog. He was helping him with his focus issues, helping him stick to a job after years of getting regularly fired...'

'Star Lord?' She couldn't suppress a chuckle.

AJ barely noticed.

'I didn't want to do it. I had enough on my plate. But the sitter cancelled on him. Anyway, long story short, that dog pulled me out of the hole I was in. Suddenly I was sleeping through the night again. Walking him three times a day forced me to start interacting with people too— dogs will make you do that. It took my mind off my grief a little. Ruby and Josiah loved him too. By the time Jamesy came back I was already looking up how to incorporate canine assistance into my own work. Then came Jetson. He took to his mission as if he knew his purpose from the start. We soon figured out how to help him communicate his findings: low blood sugar, narcolepsy, fear and stress… Dogs can pick up on tiny changes in the human body, from small shifts in our hormones to volatile organic compounds released by cancer cells. That one we're still working on. It's so varied, you know?'

Lucie realised she'd been watching his mouth throughout his whole speech, absorbing not just his words, but his energy. The same energy that had pulled *her* out of a hole, once.

She was so busy admiring him, and how nice he looked with a beard, that she missed his next words. 'Sorry, what?'

'I said, have *you* considered canine assistance? It might help you.'

'I'm not one of your patients, AJ.'

Ugh. Telling him she had nightmares had been a bad move. It wasn't as if they were even that bad. People had far bigger problems. People *she* should be out there with…helping.

'I started Thera Pups to help detect all kinds of things, as well as to help people cope.'

'I'm coping just fine,' she said stiffly.

He cocked an eyebrow. She felt bad.

'So, are many people invested in this?'

Lucie listened in awe as AJ told her as humbly

as he could how his company was already hugely successful and sparking others into the same line of work. As well as running seminars and organising conferences on the benefits of canine therapy, he had a growing number of volunteers who took dogs into nursing homes, special needs schools, hospitals…wherever they were needed.

'I've seen real healing come about because of them. Sometimes we can even arrange live-in dogs.'

'That's great,' she said, rubbing at her neck.

How the heck did a single dad with twins find time to do all of this? Was he Superman?

'But I don't need a dog—live-in or otherwise.'

AJ did not look convinced.

'I'm totally fine, really,' she pressed, flattening her palms to the table. Her skin felt clammy under his scrutiny. 'It's just the odd bad dream.'

'Well, if you change your mind, you know where I am.'

'Yes, I do,' she said, looking around for the waitress.

She offered to pay when the bill came, but AJ waved her off, swiping his card before she had time to argue.

Soon, the night air breezed around them as they walked along the silent, dark street towards the village green. AJ stopped and dropped to the wooden bench by the old stocks.

The heat rose up to her collar as he patted the seat beside him.

'Why did you think I was married to Claire?' he asked quietly, turning his face to the sky.

She stared, transfixed by his ruggedly handsome face. So different. But the familiarity of her friend from all those years ago was still there, still having the same effect on her heart.

'I guess I saw you around together,' she lied, embarrassed now. She'd been such an idiot to assume. 'I put the pieces together.'

'The wrong pieces.'

'Well, I know that now.'

AJ draped a lazy arm along the back of the bench. 'She's Belle's friend. I mean, I guess she had a crush on me a long time ago, but that's it.' He sniffed, kicked at a stone on the ground. 'I was kind of messed up, you know? When you left for America and then blocked me.'

Lucie's throat constricted. Her heart thundered in her chest. She'd messed up—abandoned him without even thinking of his wellbeing. He'd missed her, his friend, and she'd snatched her friendship away from him just because she wasn't able to have *more*. So selfish of her.

She stood quickly, shame filling her heart. What if it was showing in her eyes—the fact that she had always wanted more than his friendship? She glanced away, just in case.

'You were meant to meet Ebby, have your twins, start your business—'

'I know,' he cut in, clearing his throat, standing up. 'Obviously I know that.'

'And *I* was meant to go back to Colorado to qualify as a doctor, and then take this job with the Medicine Relief Operatives. I've never stayed in one place very long. I don't really enjoy that...'

'I know.'

They were standing inches apart under the streetlight. AJ's gaze rose from the grass up to her eyes, and she wondered if they were thinking the same thing now: *What if...? What if...? What if...?*

Every nerve in her body was shot to pieces. A compelling need came over her to lie down and close her eyes and process all this. Alone. Her emotions were piling up on top of one another, threatening to spill over.

'Well, this has been great... Thank you for inviting me, Austin,' she managed.

'So, *now* I'm Austin?' A muscle flickered in his cheek.

Lucie hugged herself. 'I'll see you around, I guess?'

'I guess you will,' she heard him mumble as she turned. 'Good that we've cleared things up.'

'Yup, absolutely. Very good.'

Cringing, she hurried on. Maybe it was hearing about Ebby, the nostalgia of the Old Ram Inn, and the village green, seeing those lips and eyes up close again, all getting to her all at once, but if she didn't move quickly—very quickly—she might turn back and kiss him.

CHAPTER FIVE

IT WAS THE weekend before Austin saw Lucie again. He knew she'd been busy working, but with her specialism in mental health he'd half expected to bump into her on his rounds at the care home. The GP practice was just steps from the hospital, too. But so far he'd not seen as much as her shadow.

Until now.

Here she was right now, studying the fresh eggs on a market stall as if they might hold the secrets of the universe.

The twins were picking out apples from the fruit stall next to him. He knew the market was busy enough that he could slip away quickly without her seeing him if he hurried them on, but...

Nope. Too late.

'Austin! Ruby, Josiah... What a day, huh? Blue sky that matches your eyes and your cooking lesson to look forward to later—am I right?'

Old Nigel, the trader behind the fruit and veg

stall, had the loudest voice known to man. Lucie's head turned in their direction.

'Hi…' she said to him, putting the box of eggs down.

Adrenaline buzzed through his belly as she crossed to him, glancing at the twins. Nigel was entertaining them with an apple juggling act. Jetson was lying under the stall, keeping guard as usual, awaiting his next command.

'Hi,' he replied. 'Long time, no see.'

'Long time…' She shifted her basket, laden with daffodils and tulips. Her gaze was directed to the twins.

'Daddy! Dad, look at Ruby!'

Austin spun around. Ruby was attempting to juggle like Nigel. When two apples plonked to the floor, he ran to try and catch one, but Jetson caught it instead. When he stood up he bumped straight into Lucie, who'd bent to grab the other one.

'Sorry,' they said at the same time, clutching their foreheads, laughing.

There she was—his Lucie. As if she'd never left.

It was obvious why he'd wanted to run just now. Just sharing the same postcode with her had him wondering things, questioning things. Feeling guilty, actually. What would people say if they knew how quickly all those unrequited feelings for Lucie had raced back in? He'd fallen for her long before he'd ever met Ebby…

'Here.' She broke his gaze, handed him the other

apple, and a moment passed where he didn't quite know what to do or say.

'I recognise you from the pub the other night,' Nigel said, shaking Lucie's hand. 'Good of you to take this one on a date. It's been a while, hey, old son?'

Austin huffed a laugh he didn't mean, avoiding Lucie's eyes. He threw fruit in a bag while they all chatted, aware of Lucie's position, how her red blouse matched her lipstick almost exactly, how hot she looked in her tight jeans.

How she kept throwing glances his way.

When a new person showed up in the village, it was all anyone talked about. Not everyone knew Lucie from before. Nigel didn't. Their history was written in their body language, though. It must be. He wasn't the same around her...he just couldn't be. Even if they'd never been more than friends, he couldn't help wondering if it was obvious how much he'd been thinking about her this past week.

Lucie carried an air of importance. She was someone people respected and admired. She'd left here to make her mark. But there was something burdened about her now—a heaviness clear to him, yet indistinct. No wonder, after what she'd seen. Her eyes looked tired as she talked with Nigel. Did she have those nightmares she'd mentioned often? Did she wake up lost and frightened, wondering if she'd ever feel normal again, like *he'd* used to...?

Nigel was called away to weigh some bananas and Ruby appeared at his side. 'Who's this, Daddy?'

A loaded question, if ever there was one.

Lucie bent down to her height and held out her hand. 'I'm Lucie. I'm an old friend of your daddy's.' She smiled warmly. 'And you must be Ruby?'

'Yes, and that's my brother Josiah.' Ruby jabbed a finger towards Josiah, who was now trying and failing to juggle apples.

'He always has to be involved in everything,' Austin explained as his mind churned with how strange it was that Lucie Henderson was here, petting his dog, talking to Ruby, who was now telling Lucie all about her plans to help him make an apple pie later, or maybe apple crumble.

'Gramma May makes the best apple crumble,' Lucie responded. 'Remember that, AJ... Austin?'

He nodded, raising an eyebrow. *Austin.*

It was almost as if her using his actual name was a new means for her to put some distance between them. Old versus new. Best friends versus almost-strangers.

Fine by him. Things *were* different now. He was a single dad. Busy. So damn busy. His schedule was rammed...and she was not here to stay.

'You know Gramma May?' Ruby frowned, trying to put the pieces together.

Austin found himself explaining the relationship between Lucie and May, and how Lucie had been away, saving lives overseas.

'*Trying* to save lives,' Lucie reminded him quietly.

Frowning, he struggled to compute the self-deprecation in her tone. A thousand lives must have been saved by her and her team over the years. The horrors she must have seen sent him cold. Since the other night he'd been thinking far too much about Lucie, and everything he'd felt compelled to let pour out of his mouth about Ebby.

It had always been pretty easy to share things with Lucie. Maybe that was why he'd told her how Ebby had died, in detail. She'd wriggled so far under his skin when he was younger that her absence had almost destroyed him...like getting a vital organ sucked out of him.

From time to time over the years he'd wondered if maybe he'd plucked up the courage and actually told her how he'd really felt about her back then, she wouldn't have moved to America... But trust her to show up now, like an upgrade, a new version of the girl who'd disappeared from his life without a backward glance.

She still had that voice that skittered along his nerve-endings, those ripe berry lips and a dusting of freckles across her nose that he hoped no make-up would ever hide. She'd had a pixie haircut when she'd left. Now her hair was long and sleek, like liquid silk. He could picture it tousled upon a pillow...

Why was he thinking about her in bed?

'Do you want to come and make apple pie with us later?' Ruby asked, and the question was loaded with hope.

What?

'Can she, Daddy? Gramma May could come too.'

Austin stared at his daughter, feeling Lucie's eyes on him. Ruby knew most people in the village. And as Lucie had cut him off, she probably had no idea what a rock May had been for them all after Ebby died.

'I'm sure Lucie and Gramma May are both very busy, sweetie. It's a Saturday,' he told Ruby diplomatically.

But then the old, familiar, unfortunate urge to make Lucie happy forced the next words from his mouth.

'Unless...unless you do find yourself at a loose end later, Lucie? Belle will be there at some point, after her shift at Lavender Springs. I know she'd love to see you. Both of you.'

'May has plans,' Lucie replied, fiddling with the tulips in her basket. 'She has more of a social life than me, you know. I've been away too long.'

'Then come by yourself. We usually start around four p.m.,' he said, cursing the kid inside him, still trying to comfort a wounded bird.

Why was he inviting her? Let alone to something he'd been doing privately in his kitchen with his kids and his sister for the years since Ebby had passed. Cooking was a kind of reset for them all…a chance to bond and talk. Just them. He'd never asked anyone to join them before.

'I guess I'll come for a bit, then,' Lucie said slowly. 'Thanks for the invite, Ruby.'

With plans made for her to call round later, Austin gathered the twins and did his best to resume what was usually the best if the most hectic time of the week. Time away from clients and meetings and seminars to spend with the twins.

But Lucie played in his head the whole time, like a song.

The past should be water under the bridge now they were grown adults. They *needed* to be OK if they were going to be bumping into each other like this, at least till she left Brookborough to work abroad again.

Lucie would never stay in one place. She loved her job too much for that. And he definitely wouldn't ever let her get close enough for another departure to faze him. But…

But what? What was the big deal in her coming over to help make a pie? It wasn't like it was a date—just like the last time hadn't been a date. Why would he want a date with Lucie, anyway?

What the hell are you doing…literally inviting the first girl to break your heart back into your life?

CHAPTER SIX

'Now, *THAT* IS how you roll pastry—love your work, Ruby-Roo!'

Lucie was struck by the love in this kitchen. The way AJ interacted with his kids was beyond cute. He was patient, encouraging, he made everything fun...and he looked damn fine in an apron.

Crayon and pencil drawings covered the whole fridge, stuck on with alphabet magnets. One was of a scruffy out-of-proportion dog, signed by Ruby. She remembered AJ's drawings had been stuck up there once.

AJ was barefoot, in jeans and a white T-shirt with *Jetson's Human* written on it, under a photo of the dog. He looked like Father of the Year in an apron, complete with floury handprints all over the front. She'd always liked him barefoot...

A couple of hours into their apple pie making session, her heart still vaulted to her throat every time he looked at her. This was weird—like living in two different worlds. The past and the present would not align in her mind.

'Taste this,' AJ said now, holding out a spoon to her over the counter.

His floury fingers clasped hers as she put them around the spoon. His eyes on her lips made the apple mixture taste strange, and the children's chatter blur into white noise. She was back by the church, the night she'd turned fourteen, pressing her finger to his in a blood oath that they'd spend every birthday together for ever. That was after Auntie Lina had forgotten her birthday.

Drawing her eyes away, she busied her hands with rolling out more pastry. They were making several pies today, with the intention of delivering some of them to the care home. At least AJ was.

She caught him sneaking glances at her. Was this weird for him too?

Ebby was here. She could hardly ignore the fact that Ebby was here, even if she'd never lived here. She was in most of the photos on the wall in the hall. The first thing Lucie had seen when she'd walked in. All curly raven hair and smiling eyes, slender arms wrapped around AJ. He'd caught her looking at the pictures for far too long. But she'd never pictured him with anyone other than herself and Claire Bainbridge.

What he must have gone through, losing Ebby...

'So, tell me more about the dogs,' she said to him, when the pies were browning nicely in the oven and the twins had been instructed to go and wash their hands.

AJ pulled out a chair at the dining table, put a cup of tea down in front of her.

'You still take extra milk, right?' he said. 'You used to like it like that—more milk than tea.'

'Still do,' she said, unable to hide her smile.

AJ slid into the chair opposite hers, sending a cloud of flour whirling around them.

'The dogs…' he said. 'Yes, I don't know what I would've done if I hadn't set up Thera Pups.'

Jetson padded out from under the table and headed for the stairs. He was responding to a playful squeal from the upstairs bathroom.

'Since the news about the disease detection programme we're developing went out, it's been full on.'

'Does it really work?' she asked, intrigued. 'I mean, can they really do that?'

'If we train them properly. I'm working on a research paper about modifying these techniques all the time, so we can pass them on. We still don't know exactly which chemical compounds for different types of cancers the dogs are sensing, for example. We can only narrow it down in time.'

'It's incredible,' she told him, feeling pride flushing through to her face as he nodded humbly, as if it wasn't even that big a deal.

'We have a long way to go, still. Did you think any more about taking on a dog while you're here, by the way?'

'Not really,' she admitted, even as her heart skittered.

Had he been serious before, about assigning her a therapy dog? Did he think she was broken because of the accident with Jorge and the dreams? Surely she didn't come off that way? Then again, he *knew* her.

But other people around here knew her, too. They cared.

What was it Gramma May had said this morning, when Lucie had joked about how nice it was to be around people who'd known her for years and liked her anyway?

'It is nice, isn't it? You can't build a community like Brookborough around you if you always have one foot out through the door.'

Gramma had a point. Lucie had missed all this a lot over the years, whenever she'd allowed herself to really think about it.

'And how are the dreams now you've been back here a while? Any less intense?'

AJ's blue-grey eyes seemed to scan her very soul, in a hundred shades of empathy. She found herself pressing her thumb to her forefinger, over the place she'd once bled into his bloodstream.

'They don't happen that often any more,' she lied.

He frowned, pressed a hand to hers, and it was hard to know whether to be touched by his kindness or offended that he clearly still thought she needed canine therapy. Even so, his concern for her forced a new road through the blocks around her heart. She hadn't let anyone in for a long time. It was surface level interactions for the most part when it came to talking about the things that really tore at her. It was better that way, for someone like her who was always on the move.

Don't go deep, don't get attached.

'What are the dreams like?' he asked quietly. 'When you do have them, I mean.'

A long moment passed between them in silence.

'Awful,' she admitted eventually, suddenly so moved by his concern and the thought of her terrible dreams that she had to blink back the moisture from her eyes.

He wouldn't *want* her to describe them even if she could.

'I know what it's like, Lucie. There were moments after Ebby died when I just—'

The key turned in the front door, cutting him off. A chorus of 'Auntie Belle!' erupted from upstairs, followed by the clattering of little footsteps.

AJ sprang from his seat. He flipped the kettle back to boil, and Lucie swiped at her face as Belle entered the kitchen.

'Lucie, hi!'

Belle hugged her, and she returned the embrace, thankful for the interruption. That had got tense so fast. How did AJ still manage to move her and open her up like a tin can? She always had get lost in his eyes. And he'd been about to confide in her something about Ebby. What?

Maybe she didn't want to know.

'It's so nice to see you! How are you?'

Belle looked the same, blonde hair swinging round her shoulders, blue-eyed and smiley, with the trademark Johnstone cheekbones Lucie would have killed for. His mum Pamela had them too. She'd loved his mum, growing up. She'd loved all of them.

'I'm great,' Lucie lied on autopilot.

AJ raised his eyebrows.

'Belle was at Lavender Springs today,' he explained next, sticking a teabag into a cup for his sister. 'She's Chief Nursing Officer there. She lets me know which patients might appreciate some time with the dogs.'

'Speaking of which,' Belle said, sinking into a chair, kicking off her shoes. 'Jack Granger had a bad day again today. He's had a stroke and now he can't use his left arm. He's a little quiet. I've a feeling his confidence has taken a knock...you can see it in his eyes...'

Lucie listened as Belle talked about the people in the care home while simultaneously fussing over the kids. They clearly worked well as a unit. But AJ was going to be here alone with the twins when Belle moved out and got married. That must be a weight on his mind. Also...what had he been about to tell her about Ebby?

Maybe she *did* want to know.

She was thinking about him far too much. Maybe it had been a mistake to come here today. If she couldn't accept even now that friendship was all he could offer her, why put her heart on the line again like this?

'What do you think?'

'Huh?'

Belle was looking at her, head cocked, biting into a slice of uncooked apple.

'I was saying, if you're free tomorrow, you should help Austin bring some pies over to the care home and check out our boy Jetson in action. I've discovered Jack had a German Shepherd once, who used to lie under his desk at work and fart all the time. I think he'd get a kick out of Jetson. Mind you, he doesn't say much. He always goes into these monologues, then shuts down, like he's worried he's taking up too much space. Apparently he lost his...'

She trailed off and Lucie drew a sharp breath. Belle had been going to say *wife*. But she had stopped herself.

The kids were still laughing at the word 'fart', tittering behind their hands. At the mention of his name Jetson had padded back into the room and promptly rested his big soft head on AJ's knee, gazing at him beguilingly. AJ stared into space.

Lucie bit hard on her cheek. 'I promised May I

would take some things to the charity shop for her tomorrow,' she said.

'That won't take you all day, will it?' Belle challenged.

'Don't pressure her, Belle, she didn't come home for this,' AJ said when she didn't reply.

Josiah wandered in from the lounge, waving a book, saying something about it being time to read to Jetson, and Belle went with him. Soon she and AJ were alone again, breathing in apple fumes in silence.

'They love reading to that dog,' he said to her eventually. 'It helps them, actually. They're advanced for their age.'

Then he shook his head, lowered his voice.

'Sorry about Belle. She's just really proud of the programme and everything Thera Pups does at the care home, you know. Wants to show everyone. You really don't have to go—'

'What were you going to tell me before?' she cut in, surprised at how badly she wanted to know. 'You said there were moments after Ebby died...'

'Oh.' AJ leaned against the counter. He pushed his hair back from his forehead, and the fine lines of time and grief etched on his skin made her want to go to him even before he spoke.

'I don't know... I was caught up in the moment. I shouldn't be telling you things about...all that.'

Her stomach dropped. 'Why not?'

AJ shrugged and turned away, rooting in the

fridge for something. He shut the fridge without retrieving anything at all, and sighed again, yanking off the apron.

'Because it's not your problem.'

Ugh. Friends were supposed to confide in each other. But then, she'd cut him off for the sake of her own stupid lovesick heart, hadn't she?

'What is my problem?' she ventured.

Surely enough water had sloshed under the bridge now for her to be his friend while she was here? It wasn't as if she'd be around for long.

'I don't want to bring you down, Lucie. You still have healing of your own to do, rather than worrying about me. It's been five whole years since Ebby died. I'm totally fine.'

She crossed to him, magnetised by his pain, and put her hand in his. He paused on the tiled floor, still holding the apron. Sparks shot right up the length of her arm.

'I don't think you can ever be totally fine, AJ,' she whispered, despite her galloping heart. 'You can start feeling better, sure…in time…but I hope you don't think it's not OK to…well, to not be OK.'

'I'm OK.'

'This is *me* you're talking to.'

It came out harsher than she'd meant it to. He stared at her for a moment, then at her hand in his, squeezing it before letting go. The lack of warmth left her cold.

'Look at us.'

He huffed a laugh she could tell he didn't mean, before draping the apron on a hook by the door and answering a call from the twins for a glass of milk.

She took a seat at the table again, defeated. *Us.* There was no 'us'. There never had been, really— not in the way she'd wanted. He probably had a hundred people to talk to in this community, so why should he want to talk to her all of a sudden? They were so far beyond being an 'us' now, it wasn't even funny—but whose fault was that? She was the one who'd pushed *him* away all these years.

It hadn't been her intention to get heavy again. It was just so easy to talk to him, and she'd stupidly assumed he felt the same. It was hard to hear about Ebby, but she wanted him to think he could talk to her.

This was so confusing.

By the time she left for Gramma May's house, full of apple pie and stories about therapy dogs, Lucie had decided it was better for both of them if she stayed away from AJ while she was here. All she'd done was complicate things for herself.

They'd be friends, maybe, while she was here. Not *close* friends. More like acquaintances. The kind of acquaintances who nodded on passing but didn't really hang out. The kind whose blood no longer ran in each other's veins.

Only that night, infuriatingly, when the dreams forced her awake in a cold sweat at three a.m., it was AJ's face, and the image of him petting Jetson, with the twins giggling in the background, that she found herself homing in on in order to calm down.

CHAPTER SEVEN

AUSTIN SETTLED ON the edge of the huge leather chair. The carpeted lounge smelled like coffee and air freshener, and in the background a nursing assistant was doing the rounds with a plate of biscuits. Jack Granger, the eighty-nine-year-old stroke victim, was sitting up rigidly in the chair opposite, watching Jetson roll a ball around the floor. Jack refused a biscuit when offered. His long, drawn face and sad, hooded eyes told Austin he was still grieving the loss of his wife as well as the use of his arm.

Belle had mentioned last week, when he'd come into Lavender Springs with the apple pies, that Jack had taken a while to warm up to her, but Austin had hoped that bringing Jetson back again today might scored him bonus points with the man.

No such luck. This was Austin's second visit to Jack, and he'd had barely a peep out of him. He'd hoped Lucie might have taken Belle up on her offer to visit last week too, but she hadn't. He hadn't seen her since, but he'd seen the car she'd hired around.

'How's your arm doing today?' he asked Jack now, before he could dwell on the fact that she wasn't going to go out of her way to be around him—not after all these years. She had better things to do with her time than hang out with a single dad and his dogs.

Jack sighed dejectedly at his question. 'Same as every day. Useless. Can't even tie my own shoes.'

Austin glanced at the old man's feet. 'You're wearing slippers.'

Jack's thin mouth twitched. 'Doesn't mean I wouldn't wear lace-ups if I could. Can you train a dog to tie shoelaces?'

'Not yet...but let me work on that.'

Austin threw the ball for Jetson, who promptly retrieved it and placed it at Jack's feet, panting hopefully. A wistful look crossed his deeply lined face now, almost as if a memory of a better time was playing out in his head...something he didn't want to voice out loud.

They sat in silence for a while. The ball went untouched. Then Austin said, 'I hear you had a German Shepherd once?'

Jack nodded. 'Shadow,' he croaked. 'She went everywhere with me. That was years ago. Before I met my Alice. Never could replace that dog.'

Austin threw the ball for Jetson again. This

wasn't about him, but anyone who'd lost his wife had his full sympathy. 'Didn't Alice like dogs?'

'She did. But she didn't want anything to compete for my attention,' Jack replied. 'Later, she said the more she got to know me, the more she wanted to get a dog after all. I never did know quite how to take that.'

Austin couldn't help a chuckle, which Jack seemed to reciprocate behind a weathered hand. To his surprise, when Jetson deposited the ball back at his feet Jack reached for it with his good arm and threw it across the room.

Jetson raced after it, tail wagging, causing one lady in another chair to lift her legs and laugh. Austin stood up to apologise, right as someone tapped him on the shoulder from behind his chair.

'Belle!'

'Hey, little brother, look who I found.'

His sister was all smiles in her pale pink uniform, no doubt impressed by this tiny bit of dog-influenced progress on Jack's part. And there was someone with her.

'Lucie,' he said, blinking back the shock of her sudden appearance.

Lucie was wearing the hell out of a fitted black pencil skirt and a high-necked blouse, and the same blazer she'd worn that night to the Old Ram Inn. Pink lipstick and pink blusher, hair styled and straightened…she was already catching attention in the care home. Maybe they thought she was a celebrity.

Jetson sat before them, waiting to be allowed to greet them, and Austin watched as Lucie patted his head, somewhat awkwardly at first, then with more enthusiasm.

'I didn't know you'd be here with Jack today,' she told him, holding her hand out to Jack, who took it.

Jack looked a little taken aback by her, so immaculately dressed and beautiful. He took off his glasses to study her.

Lucie introduced herself. She was obviously here for an assessment. Jack was registered with the GP practice, of course.

Austin pulled up another chair for her, wishing his heartrate hadn't skyrocketed through the care home's ceiling. Some warning might have been nice, he thought, as the back of his neck prickled with heat under his shirt collar.

Belle excused herself and hurried back towards Reception.

Lucie cleared her throat, eyeing Austin's lanyard with a small smirk.

Jack looked between them with interest. 'You two know each other?'

'A little,' Lucie admitted.

'I'd wager more than just a little,' Jack said, and smirked.

Austin crossed his arms and Lucie mirrored

him, then caught herself and pressed her hands back to her sides.

'What makes you say that?' she asked.

'I can just tell. Your eyes lit up when you saw her,' he said to Austin. 'My arm might not work, but my eyes do.'

'We used to be friends,' Austin said.

Lucie squared her shoulders. He couldn't read her face as she took her seat, but he sensed annoyance radiating from her. He should probably take his leave, let her do her thing, but Jetson had sat obediently at her feet, as if he, too, wanted to know what came next. This was more than Jack had spoken before, ever, which was one good thing, he supposed.

'Right, then...' Austin clapped his hands together and looked around for some other topic of conversation that wouldn't put them both on the spot. He couldn't seem to find one.

His eyes had *not* lit up. Had they?

It was just that his mind had somehow spun him back to that time when she'd appeared from nowhere at the dance when they were ten—just shown up in the school gym under the balloons, the most gorgeous girl he'd ever seen. That was the moment he'd realised he had feelings for a girl.

He'd stood on her toes more than once that night, but he'd bought her a bar of chocolate and she'd pretended not to care. That had been two weeks before they'd kissed on the bridge. He'd known then that she wasn't like the other girls. Lucie had made things wake up inside him. He'd never told her. What if she'd laughed at him? Or wanted nothing more to do with him?

That had been the start of him hiding his feelings from her, keeping their friendship sacred above everything else.

'We knew each other a long time ago,' Lucie said carefully. 'I used to live near here, actually. I've just come back to Brookborough for a while, and I thought I'd see what crazy stuff you're all getting up to at Lavender Springs.'

She went on to explain how her late grandfather had been a resident here, prior to his death, how *he'd* never had any visits from dogs, and how much her family had always loved dogs yet she'd never had one.

Austin felt a flush of pride as she added that she'd been encouraged to read more about canine assistance over the last week or so because of *him*.

She didn't mention her nightmares. Were they still torturing her? Was *that* what had brought her here, finally? The hope that there might be something out there to help aside from some time spent at Gramma May's?

He'd thought a lot about what might be haunting Lucie's dreams—someone close to her had died right in front of her. What had she seen, exactly? The way she dressed... It was almost as if she was trying to be someone else now—someone who hadn't seen all that tragedy.

Soon, it seemed that Jack had clean forgotten Austin was there at all. Somehow Lucie had got him talking more about his German Shepherd, Shadow. He watched her as she listened, assessing his mind, seeing how it worked, what he did and didn't react and respond to. But the whole time Austin found himself trying to decipher what was really going on in *her* mind. He'd used to know her so well and now…whether his eyes lit up around her or not…they were strangers.

He'd pulled away, he supposed. On purpose that time at the house, when she'd asked him about Ebby. Well, it wouldn't exactly be fair to load all his issues on her when she had enough of her own problems, but she'd kept away ever since, and he'd convinced himself she wanted nothing more to do with him.

Maybe he'd scared her off…inviting her to a house filled with photos of Ebby. Lucie had used to view that house as being as much her own as his, and now it was a shrine to a person she'd never even met.

Hang on. As if that was *his* fault.

He prickled, noting how, not for the first time since her return, he was wondering how his life might have played out if he'd told her how he'd felt about her. Would she never have left? Would he not have wound up with Ebby? The thought caused his insides to itch. With just his thoughts alone he was betraying Ebby. The mother of his children.

Jack was asking her why he'd never seen her around before.

'I'm a locum. I'm on a bit of a break from my regular job.'

'Why?' Jack asked.

Lucie paused.

Austin jumped in. 'She'll be back at it soon enough, don't you worry, Jack. Lives on the other side of the world, this one. We can't keep her here. I doubt anyone can.'

Lucie forced a smile, but her eyes narrowed. 'No one ever *tried* to keep me here,' she said coolly.

Austin fiddled with his collar as Jack cocked his head in interest.

Maybe she was right. But even if he *had* told her his real feelings, nothing would have stopped Lucie Henderson from doing what she wanted to do.

Why was he so annoyed with her all over again simply for being *Lucie*? The past was history. It wasn't as if she was trying to insert herself into his life again, only to mess him up a second time. He *knew* she was leaving again—and so did she— and he was totally one hundred percent fine with that. They'd hardly seen each other anyway, since she'd got here.

Yeah, but you've been thinking about her... And just knowing she's around is enough to rock your foundations. That's why you're being snarky.

'Well…' Jack sniffed. 'God bless the work you both do with people like me. Rest of the world might've given up, but…' He winced as he tried to move his arm.

Austin was out of his seat in a flash, arranging a cushion to rest on his lap. Jetson took the chance to lick Jack's hand in moral support, while Lucie tucked a blanket over his knees. Austin's hand caught her fingers across the soft fabric and she pulled her fingers away as if he'd stung her, and tossed the ball for Jetson a little too hard across the floor.

OK. She was clearly annoyed with him for that last comment. He could feel it. He'd have to apologise now.

CHAPTER EIGHT

'WHAT HAPPENED IN THERE?' Lucie faced him the second they were standing in the oak-panelled corridor. Her smile had been convincing enough for Jack—probably—but AJ's words had been pretty loaded back there.

'We can't keep her here. I doubt anyone can.'

It was true, she supposed, but hearing him say it had struck a nerve.

'I don't know why I said that,' he admitted straight away, to his credit. 'I'm sorry for how that came out. I suppose I felt a little put out that I haven't heard from you or seen you since you came to my house last week.'

Lucie sucked in a breath. A woman rolled past in a wheelchair with her carer and both of them patted Jetson's head. She and AJ forced a smile in their direction.

'Well, I'm sorry for being distant,' she whispered when they'd gone. 'I didn't really know if I should be initiating these...what are they? Meetups? You're busy with the twins, and all *this*, and I'm busy at the practice…'

'It's not that, though, is it?' he said.

Her stomach bucked.

'It's weird,' he went on. 'For both of us. Being around each other again. We might as well admit it. I thought the pie-making session would be nice, but…'

'It *was* nice.'

'But it freaked you out…seeing me as a dad, being in that house again.'

Lucie pursed her lips. 'OK, fine. Seeing you as a dad was a little weird. Not *bad*, just…'

'Not what you expected to come home to?' he offered.

Smoothing the seams of her pencil skirt, she avoided his eyes, waiting for him to continue. She had felt strange around him in a house full of Ebby's pictures—especially when her feelings were bubbling up all over again. Feelings for an ex best friend and now widower she could never have. But she wasn't going to admit that part. And, anyway, why should he feel weird around her? Hadn't he got happily married and forgotten all about her?

'I can't just forget that you left without even telling me—without even saying goodbye or discussing that offer from your aunt to go to America.'

He cast his eyes to hers, squared his shoulders. She held her breath.

'What happened?' he asked.

'I was always relying on you, AJ. I had to do something for myself. Things got busy…and you know what it's like when you're eighteen. It's all about yourself at that age.'

Her smile felt brittle, even to herself. Her excuse sounded weak and heartless, but better to keep his mind from jumping on the fact that she'd been deluded back then, thinking he might ask her to stay. Even if he hadn't hooked up with Claire, he'd never have been hers. He'd only ever seen her as a friend.

'I do know what it's like being eighteen,' he said now. 'I spent the year wondering where the hell you were.'

'I'm sorry,' she managed.

She really was. And deeply ashamed to have been such a terrible friend.

'Well, I'm sure you were a great success in America,' he said next. 'And I don't just mean professionally.'

He looked at her askance. Was he was waiting for her to divulge intel on her dating life?

Lucie pulled a face. As if she'd tell him that she'd had just two relationships in her life—both with team members out in the field, neither of which had lasted. Probably because she'd packed her suitcase and said, 'See ya later,' the second they'd hinted that they might want to leave the MRO and 'settle down and have kids some day' with her.

This was getting awkward. He knew something

was off because he knew *her*. But it would be even more awkward if she admitted she'd had a giant stinking crush on him once. He might even think she wanted to start something up with him now.

He was a father, for goodness' sake! And *she* had the itchiest feet on earth. Also, no fixed address to speak of. That was hardly the recipe for a stable, doting mother figure, was it? If there was one thing she knew about parenting, it was that she knew nothing at all. How *could* she, having been raised by her grandparents? Stable, devoted, and loving as they'd been, they hadn't been her mum and dad.

They'd barely talked about her parents—as if they'd been afraid it might upset her, and consequently *them*. And as for Aunt Lina—well, there was a woman with even itchier feet than hers. For all her good intentions and generous financial support, Lina had always been more like a busy older sister, who'd invite you to things, then forget she'd ever asked and leave without you.

'I'm not here to drag up the past, AJ. My past here or anywhere else,' she told him measuredly, trying not to bristle as her own maternal impairments and misgivings seemed to rain down upon her head like waste from a space station.

She was probably everything AJ did not need in his life right now. Josiah and Ruby needed stability. Someone they could count on.

'OK, but, I was hoping we could be friends again,' he said in response. 'Start afresh?'

'I'd love it if we could be friends again,' she said, before she could think about it too much.

He took her stuck-out hand and shook it in an exaggerated manner that left her wondering if he remembered the blood oath they'd made. *'You'll always be in my blood, Lucie.'* That was what he'd said.

'So what's your verdict on Jack?' he asked her, changing the subject as he led her to another door along the corridor.

She caught the North Yorkshire Moors and Yorkshire Dales Dark Skies Festival posters along the way, all the framed photos and platitudes that accentuated the caring vibe. It was nice in here. But growing old alone, with no one to visit you or care for you… She shuddered at the thought.

'You can't build a community like Brookborough around you if you always have one foot out through the door.'

Composing herself, she forced this new 'friendship' idea to settle, as if it was a disobedient puppy, bouncing around between them.

'Well, he's still grieving. That will slow his physical healing. But I can see the dog is helping. Like I said, I've been reading about canine assistance…'

'And how it might help your dreams?'

'I wouldn't go that far.'

Of course he knows.

'OK, fine…' She sighed. 'I'd rather have Freddy Kreuger slip into my dreams than the stuff I see sometimes when I close my eyes. I thought maybe if I dipped a toe into your world—' She caught herself, catching his eyes. 'Your world of *dogs*,' she asserted, 'and how they can help with mental health in various capacities, I might at least learn something new while I keep myself busy in this role. You don't mind, do you, if I schedule some of my appointments at the same time as yours? Shadow you sometimes?'

'That depends.'

Here we go.

'On what?'

'Whether you're good with dogs.'

He nudged her. She rubbed her shoulder, stepping away and hesitating before responding. 'I guess I'll find out.'

Why was she feeling so nervous? AJ's gaze held hers, and for a moment she felt he could see right through her, and she through him. Was there something there, between them?

Don't be stupid. It's just wishful thinking…a throwback emotion from your childhood.

She bit her cheek as he offered to come with her to her next patient and bring Jetson along, seeing as he had an hour between appointments. She agreed, of course. Starting again as friends was the only way they could work together, and even though it was slightly uncomfortable, it did feel good to clear the air somewhat.

And maybe there really were a few things to learn from having him around for some of her appointments and vice versa. As long as they kept it strictly work-related, she reminded herself. No more visiting his house or hanging out with his kids—as if they'd want to hang out with her anyway. They'd probably forgotten her already.

She'd have to take a little gift for them next time...

Wait... What? There wasn't going to be a next time!

Lucie's next patient was seventy-seven-year-old Phyllis. She was sitting rather dejectedly in a soft pink high-backed chair when Lucie took a seat, offering her a kind smile. Phyllis was suffering with Parkinson's disease, and as a result often felt anxious and depressed. Her eyes moved quickly to Jetson, however, when AJ and the Labrador padded in after her.

'Who is this?' Phyllis asked.

AJ stuck out his hand. Phyllis's own hand trembled as she took it, but Lucie didn't miss how her eyes had lit up the second they entered the room.

'I'm Austin, and this is Dr Jetson,' he told her.

Lucie bit back a smile as Phyllis raised a grey eyebrow, seemingly amused. Jetson jumped onto his hind legs and placed his two front paws on the arm of her chair, as if to introduce himself.

'Did you bring my daughter with you?' Phyllis asked the dog with a smile, and then continued to have a sweet one-sided conversation with Jetson, patting his head with a shaky hand. 'You can tell I miss my grandchildren, can't you, boy? Oh, you have such a soft head…like my grandson. Just look at you…'

AJ beamed and Lucie couldn't help but smile. His enthusiasm for helping people through their bond with dogs was palpable, and she felt her heart expand another few inches, just watching him with her patient.

'We're here to talk about how we can help you, Phyllis,' Lucie said softly. 'Dr Johnstone has a special interest in dog-assisted therapy, and he has some ideas on how to incorporate it into your treatment.'

Phyllis nodded, but seemed unsure. 'I don't have time to walk a dog,' she said, as Jetson got back into a sitting position at her feet, panting lightly.

'Oh, don't you worry about that—Dr Johnstone does all the walking,' Lucie told her, and AJ performed a mock salute. Lucie leaned forward, touched Phyllis's arm lightly. 'I was thinking it could be beneficial for all of us to have some kind of collaborative treatment plan…working together with Jetson around here. He could do with some help that doesn't require walking. He really likes being read to.'

She glanced at AJ, who was mirroring her stance, resting his elbows on his knees, looking at her in something like awe or amusement. She'd already told him how Phyllis had used to love reading but was now finding it hard to focus due to her anxiety and her physical ailments. Something about hearing him say how the twins were better at reading thanks to their reading to Jetson had started her thinking. Maybe it would help Phyllis regain some of her focus and get her confidence back, too.

'What kind of things do you like to read, Jetson?' Phyllis asked now, with a slight smirk.

She motioned to AJ to hand her a couple of books from the stack by her head, which he did on command. Within minutes Lucie and AJ were both watching in fascination as Phyllis recited a page from *Moby Dick* to a bright-eyed Jetson, without faltering once.

'Some people think animals can communicate better than humans with people with dementia and Parkinson's,' AJ told her later, when a nurse came in for a quick check on Phyllis's lunch order. 'Animals rely more on body language than verbal communication.'

Lucie nodded. 'I can see that.'

She was beyond thrilled to see Phyllis responding so well to Jetson. The elderly woman was really starting to open up, and they'd both listened intently, taking notes and making suggestions as a team. Strangely, it felt natural working so closely with AJ.

As the session progressed, Phyllis began to relax slowly but surely, so much so that even her hands had less of a tremble—Lucie was sure of it.

It hadn't been planned, but somehow she knew this was the right way to go, the best way to help Phyllis. Her mental health depended on her keeping her autonomy and independence, and knowing a dog appreciated her company was somehow almost as remedial as having her grandson and her daughter there.

As for AJ—the man had the patience of a saint. He was looking impossibly handsome today, in a green woollen sweater and smart black jeans. As for her own pencil skirt and heels… She was probably overdressed, but it was imperative that she was seen as someone who was well put together—at least on the outside.

Watching him pick up the conversation with Phyllis now, she took a deep breath to calm her thoughts. His body language wasn't out of the ordinary around her. Although there were still moments when he stood too close, then corrected himself. Jack had definitely noticed something was up. Had AJ's eyes really lit up when he'd seen her? She hadn't noticed—she'd been too busy maintaining an air of indifference at seeing *him*. But then, when they were kids, he'd always seemed pretty happy being around her. Maybe she'd forgotten that…too busy being offended over something he hadn't even done with Claire!

Lucie studied AJ's every movement now—the way he interacted so kindly and patiently with Phyllis, and with Jetson, and with her.

When she went with him to his next two appointments, he introduced her as a friend.

It was what she'd wanted, after all.

He pressed some dog treats into her hand at one point, and taught her how to command Jetson to roll over, and as they laughed at the dog's antics she could see with her own eyes how Jetson's presence eased the mood. It was the same in every room.

If only he could ease hers.

It *was* what she'd wanted.

Something else was niggling at her. The look on AJ's face, when he'd suggested she must've had a boyfriend or ten over the years.

That *one* look had told her the thought of those other boyfriends affected him somehow.

Not that it should matter, she reminded herself quickly.

It was definitely best to keep this professional and not spend any more time with him than necessary, she decided, listening to him explaining to another elderly patient how Josiah and Ruby made homemade dog treats for Jetson from sweet potato and minced meat.

God, he really was Father of the Year.

Damn him for turning out so perfect. In a way, it might've been better if he *had* hooked up with Claire-bloody-Bainbridge—at least then she could still be angry with him instead of impossibly attracted.

Every time AJ caught her eye he looked away quickly, as if he'd been caught doing something illicit. It made her blood race. Maybe she wasn't imagining it. Maybe there was something there.

No...stop doing this to yourself, Lucie!

She had to stop telling herself that she and Austin Johnstone could be something more than friends. It would only lead to heartache, and that was the last thing she'd come here looking for.

CHAPTER NINE

AUSTIN CALLED THE twins to the kitchen counter, scooping cornflakes into two bowls. 'Get your own spoons. I'm late!'

In seconds the kitchen resounded with the crunch of cereal and talk about the mummies in the book they'd read last night, while Jetson waited patiently for whoever dropped a cornflake to the floor first.

Where was Gramma May? She was supposed to be here by now to look after the twins. She helped him out sometimes on Sunday mornings. Belle was off doing wedding-related things with Bryce—their Halloween wedding seemed ages away to him, but Belle insisted it would come around fast—and he had a meeting with the volunteers about the upcoming Paws Under the Stars event. He was supposed to be heading it up himself. Starting now.

The doorbell rang. *Thank goodness*. Yanking it open, he swiped up his car keys, ready to dash, but it wasn't Gramma May.

'Lucie?'

She straightened and dashed a manicured hand through the ponytail slung over her left shoulder. Her hair disappeared into the folds of a soft white scarf peppered with roses that matched her red down jacket and navy-blue jeans.

'Gramma May's sick,' she explained. 'Nothing serious, just a cold, but she should stay at home. I offered to cover.'

Austin pulled his eyes from her scarf. Her perfume consumed him, throwing him off. 'Are you sure?'

The twins had run to the door now, in a chorus of, 'Lucie, Lucie, come and see our fort upstairs!'

And while Lucie agreed and smiled, and patted Jetson happily in front of them, he knew better.

Why would she want to stay in his house all morning? She hadn't been over since the time they'd made apple pies. They'd done nothing together that hadn't been at the care home or the hospital for a week. Which was fine by him. But he couldn't exactly turn her away, for the twins' sake. They'd think it was weird—they liked her. Only yesterday Ruby had asked when they'd be seeing Lucie again.

'I have a better idea,' he said, before he could change his mind. 'Why don't we all go?'

Twenty minutes later they were climbing out of the car at Newman's Farm in Malton. He watched

Lucie take a lungful of the cool morning air, soaking up the views.

'It's beautiful! I forgot how magical everything looks in this light.'

He watched the sun glinting temptingly off her lip gloss. The taste of her lips would no doubt drive him wild if he ever kissed her. He'd kissed her once, he remembered, but he'd been so young he hadn't even known what to do with the feelings such intimacy had elicited.

'This is halfway to where the event will be held at Gilling Castle,' he said, locking the car. 'One of my volunteers runs the tearoom here, and the dogs can run free.'

The twins ran ahead with Jetson, towards the children's farm area, while he walked with Lucie after them. Her eyes shone with nostalgia as she took it all in: the dogs running around, the clucking chickens, the thatched roof farmhouse, the organic vegetable gardens, the weeping willow trees lining the paddocks of sheep and horses.

'Bit different to Nepal' he said.

She looked to the ground. He kicked himself for saying that. It had probably cast a downer on her train of thought, dragging her mind back to the earthquake.

The kids were already knee-deep in hay. They were making a fuss over their favourite goat as he leaned on the fence at the side of the pen with Lucie.

'I'll stay with them while you go and meet the others,' she offered.

OK… It wasn't as if he'd be putting her out. There wasn't much for her to do really, except stand there looking gorgeous and untouchable with the sun in her hair.

Her foot landed in a pile of goat poop the second she stepped into the pen. Darting in, Austin steadied her by her elbow, watching the look of torture in her eyes at both the contact and the poop, before she cursed under her breath and made the twins snort.

'Shi… Shoot!' She grimaced, scraping her boot on a fence post.

The twins just cracked up even more.

'Now *you* both have to stand in some poop, so I'm not the only one,' she joked at them, eyeing Austin sideways.

Ruby and Josiah took it literally and stomped in the hay in their welly boots, shouting, *'Poop dance!'*

'They don't care what they stand in,' he told her.

Lucie looked at them, aghast, then at him, before breaking out into laughter. The sound of it drew him in like a warm fire.

He was still holding her elbow.

Realising it at the same time, she broke apart from him.

Something sad shuddered through him. A memory he'd long forgotten. Lucie had used to cry a lot, back when she'd first arrived in Brookborough. Sometimes she'd cry in the middle of laughing and hide her face. She'd never said why. She'd always denied it afterwards, acted tough, but he'd been drawn to that inner flame. Like a moth tapping on a window…trying to get to the light.

'Daddy!'

Ruby's shriek pierced his skull. He spun to her. 'Oh, Ruby, what have you done?'

Her braid had somehow got caught on the fence. Before he could even act Lucie was at her side, kneeling in the hay, oblivious to the filth.

She worked it out with her fingers, hushing her till Ruby stilled, soothed by her calm conviction. His own redundancy should have stung, but the scene of motherly care moved him. Lucie had patiently detangled Ruby's hair and smoothed it down, told her she was fine, that she'd just done too much enthusiastic 'poop dancing'.

'Thank you,' he said to her, thinking, *Ebby would have done that.*

Why was he busy putting halos around Lucie's head when he should be thinking of Ebby? Guilt-ridden thoughts like this had messed his head up ever since he'd carried Lucie out of that stream. Ebby had been his world, but a tiny part of him recognised that he'd loved Lucie harder, with more of himself.

If Lucie had never left, he might not have even met Ebby. Maybe his feelings would have got the better of him eventually, and he'd have told Lucie he'd been in love with her in silence for years. Maybe she would've rejected him outright. But he was starting to wonder if maybe she wouldn't…

'I know what it's like to get your hair caught,' she replied now, biting back a smile, brushing the hay and dirt from her jeans. 'Once I got mine stuck, climbing through a briar patch to rescue a koala after a flood. You don't want to mess with the brambles in Western Australia. The koala had rescued itself by the time I was free.'

Austin stared at her. She was from a whole other world now.

'I'll watch them now—you guys go.'

Sarah, the sister of one of his volunteers, had brought two kids of her own. Austin nodded his thanks as the four kids acted out the dramatic, long-winded handshake they'd memorised last time they'd met, sending the chickens scattering.

'Be good,' he told the twins, and turned to Lucie. 'You're off the hook with the children.'

He couldn't help his hand on her lower back as they both walked away, though he removed it as they neared the cluster of people congregating outside the tearoom.

'I didn't mind being on it,' she told him absently, still cleaning her boots in the grass.

He wanted to tell her his kids thought she was hilarious. But for the same reason he'd moved his hand, he kept his mouth shut.

They were doing OK at being friends again after all these years of estrangement, and they'd been working well as a team with Jetson at the care home and the hospital all week, but it was all a lie. He was pretending he could be close to her without stirring up memories of how she'd used to look at him as a girl. Maybe he'd missed something back then, when he'd been all teenage gangly limbs and libido and ego. She was the one girl he'd sworn never to touch, never to ruin. She'd been through enough already. So he'd busied himself with other girls to try and stop himself wanting *her*.

Much as he was still doing now.

There were lines you shouldn't cross with someone who was just passing through, he reminded himself. No way was he getting left again like Ebby had left him, standing at the window, wondering when she'd come home. *If* she'd come home.

But it *was* kind of nice to know he could feel things for someone after Ebby. Before Lucie had showed up again, it had felt as if he never would.

CHAPTER TEN

AJ's VOLUNTEER GROUP were a smiley-looking bunch—mostly women from the surrounding towns and villages.

Lucie was introduced as his friend again. Fine. It was the right thing now—although he was saying it a little too much, if she was honest. If she didn't know better she'd think he was trying to convince himself of something more than anyone else. Maybe he still hadn't quite forgiven her for walking out on their friendship with no explanation.

Before, his eyes had been fully on her when she was with Ruby. Suddenly she hoped she hadn't crossed some kind of line, putting herself in the position of a mother figure...

The not-so-secret stares from him were a new thing too. He'd been doing it all week. Admittedly, she'd been shooting him a few of her own—sizing him up, trying to force her brain to create a new impression of him, one without all the memories of her lusting over him attached. It was still amazing to her that he was a father and a widower and a much-loved member of the community…and even fitter than he had been before.

Stupid, really. He'd just grown up and built a life, like she had, but their two worlds were colliding in her mind. It was hard to separate the boy she'd loved from the man who'd never love her back. Maybe if she hadn't overheard him with Claire she might have someday gathered up the courage to tell him how she felt. Show him, perhaps?

Oh, who was she kidding? The thought of his rejection had always been crippling. Much like now, actually.

She'd almost refused to come here with him. Was it too intimate? Going on an outing with him and the twins?

Ugh…whatever. It wasn't as if they'd planned it. She'd rather this than staying at the house with images of his dead wife everywhere. And the twins were growing on her. They were funny. Interesting, she mused, how amusing kids could be without even trying.

The group were now gathered in the cosy oak-beamed tearoom, chatting amongst themselves. Some of the dogs were sitting quietly and patiently at their owners' feet, while others were sniffing around chair-legs.

One dog bounded straight up to her and sat

promptly at her feet, awaiting a pat: a sandy-brown Retriever called Maple.

Her owner laughed in surprise, getting up to greet Lucie. 'She doesn't usually do that.' The striking black woman's raven bob cut swayed around her jaw as she spoke. 'She must like you.'

'She's adorable!'

'Shame I can't keep her much longer,' the other woman said ruefully, placing a hand to the Retriever's soft head. 'My daughter's coming back from university soon, and she's allergic. We'll need to find a new foster home for her. I was only meant to keep her till now, but I've grown so attached.'

'Oh, no, poor Maple…' Lucie pouted. 'And poor you. I hope you can find someone locally, so you can still see each other.'

'So do I.'

The dog placed a fuzzy padded paw into Lucie's hand, stared up at her and stuck her tongue out. She saw AJ smile. His hand found her lower back for just a fraction of a second as he leaned in. His scent caught her off guard. He smelled like the house and fresh linen…and a little bit like goats now too. She swallowed.

'I think she's trying to ask you something,' he whispered into the shell of her ear.

Lucie couldn't look away from the dog's big brown eyes. She was beautiful, and AJ's proximity was throwing her for a loop.

'No,' she said to him firmly, coming to her senses.

'No, what?'

'I know what you're thinking. I'm not fostering a dog.'

'Lucie Henderson?'

Lucie spun around at the sound of her name, and AJ stopped his chuckling.

'Jamesy Abbot?' she cried, taking in the boy she'd known from school, still with the same blond streaked hair. His Golden Retriever, Star Lord, sniffed butts with Maple as they hugged briefly. He was obviously one of the volunteers.

Jamesy looked curiously between her and AJ. 'He said you were back. It's good to see you two together again.'

He grinned as he emphasised 'together', and Lucie looked to the floor. Typical Jamesy, stirring things up—some things never changed. He'd teased her once, about following AJ around, pointing out her crush. Had he ever asked AJ if he thought she had a crush on him?

As if it matters.

AJ excused himself, leaving her standing awkwardly between Maple's owner Iris, Jamesy, and a doting Maple, while he faced the group. He was quick to get down to business, taking the lead, commanding attention with one clap of his hands.

They were apparently sorting out the order of things for something called the Paws Under the

Stars event. He was planning the evening as part of the Spring Gala.

The volunteers were going to dress their dogs in LED lights and fantastical costumes and get them to complete an assault course and perform various tricks. Lots of dog-related merchandise was here on display, from dog harnesses to food bowls, to printed T-shirts with the Thera Pups logo on them.

'We have everything but the new calendar good to go,' AJ explained. 'We need to organise that soon, as people always ask for them early. Sometimes I think they just like to look at the photos for longer.'

It was all being done to raise money for some of the establishments they visited, and for some of the volunteers who needed a little support in caring for their animals. Some of them were only fostering, like Iris was doing with Maple.

They were deep into enthusiastic discussion when several of the dogs towards the back of the room began to whine. Lucie exchanged a curious glance with AJ, who looked only mildly concerned. Maybe they were bored, or hungry, she mused.

Then, out of nowhere, there was a thud at the back of the room.

'John!' someone yelled.

Some of the dogs were barking now, others still

whining. Lucie hurried over to the collapsed man, now grappling to hold on to a chair-leg on the tiled floor.

'He just said he didn't feel well,' said the woman who'd yelled his name. 'He has seizures. He's on meds for them, but…'

'John, can you hear me?' AJ said beside her, as the rest of the crowd stood around, hands over their mouths in shock.

John was pulsating on the floor now, cold to the touch. Looking to AJ, Lucie brought the man's head onto her lap, blocking out the rest of the room. AJ was already rummaging through John's bag for his medication and she knew they'd have to administer it right away—John's eyes were having trouble staying open.

'We've got you, John,' she soothed, hoping she was right as AJ readied the needle and passed it to her.

The man's body loosened up almost instantly. He stopped convulsing and the crowd let out thankful moans as AJ stood, ushering them back to give John space.

Someone handed her some blankets and she gently laid them over John, watching the colour seeping slowly back into his pale cheeks. He was drifting in and out of consciousness and complaining of dizziness now. At least he could speak.

She'd never been so grateful for AJ's calming presence.

* * *

Gramma May called AJ when they were halfway home.

'Gramma May is calling *you*?' she said in surprise.

He ignored her. 'I guess you heard about John?' he said into the speakerphone, and Lucie listened as the two discussed the event, and how John had thankfully been able to walk away not even twenty minutes later, thanks to AJ's quick actions.

Gramma May thanked them both, in fact, for helping her friend. She knew John and his wife from church.

'And how are *you* feeling now?' AJ asked her.

The kids called out, 'Hi, Gramma May!' from the back seat.

Gramma May insisted it was just the sniffles and not to worry.

How sweet, Lucie thought, that she'd called AJ like this, to thank him, before even calling her. They must be closer than he'd let on...closer than Gramma May had let on all these years.

Community. She'd really missed this.

She caught him as they exited the car and the kids ran ahead with the house key.

'AJ...' she said quietly.

It was hitting her now, just how out of her depth she was, coming back here. He scanned her eyes, and the intensity in them turned her stomach over. She wanted to apologise for asking Gramma May not to tell her anything about him. It must have been so hard for her to keep silent. But something stopped her. She'd been a burden to poor Gramma May even *after* she'd left home and given her her freedom, which wasn't something she was proud of—it would be best to apologise to Gramma herself.

'That was… Well, I'm glad you were there,' she told him instead.

'I'm glad you were there too,' he replied.

The intensity of the moment had her feeling awkward, and he was chewing the side of his lip.

'The twins want to know if you want to come in for a cup of tea,' he said.

For a second she considered that maybe *he* wanted her to come in, more than the twins. Torn, she gave a little sigh. It was probably best if she didn't go into the house and be reminded of all the times she'd watched him while she was meant to be watching a movie, wishing he would kiss her. Or, she reasoned, she could just act like the adult she was and have a simple cup of tea.

She ended up staying all afternoon.

Leaving was near impossible.

Every time she got up, the twins had something else to show her: Ruby's puzzle collection, the way AJ had an ongoing skipping rope competition going with Josiah in the living room. It was sexy as hell, that one, watching him jump just to make his kids laugh.

When she finally had the tiniest moment alone with AJ inside the fort, made of cotton sheets in all the colours AJ wouldn't put on the bed, her knee brushed his for a thousandth of a second . She could have launched herself on him.

'Sorry,' she said instead.

His breath warmed her neck when he laughed, and a groan lingered in her throat that she had to swallow back.

AJ hugged his knees.

She almost...*almost* asked him if he'd ever considered asking her out all those years ago. He'd asked all those other girls out—why not her, ever? But that wasn't like her. That was way too needy, wasn't it? And neediness was not her thing. She'd leave that to the dogs. Instead, she asked him how on earth the dogs had seemed to know what was about to happen to John earlier, before anyone had seen the signs.

Why look for ways to attach herself to him and these two delightful little energy balls he'd somehow raised without his wife? she thought, admiring his mouth, and the passion with which he answered her about dogs' infinite intelligence and potential, and the paper he was writing.

He'd done so much—buried his roots so far into the ground here. While she was still a bird, aiming for the mountaintops. Literally. She was probably just feeling emotional after what had happened today, that was all. She'd never be the kind of woman he needed now—not even if she tried.

Somehow, that hurt more than she wanted to admit.

CHAPTER ELEVEN

THE BLOND-HAIRED BOY'S eyes widened anxiously when Austin entered the room with Jetson. He'd decided to involve him for his second attempted Autism Spectrum Disorder assessment on eleven-year-old Jake, who had refused all attempts to so much as question him till now.

'You brought a dog?' he said suspiciously, folding his arms across the desk he was sitting behind in the quiet room at the GP practice that doubled as Austin's office for appointments like this.

His mother was already on her feet, patting Jetson, encouraging Jake to do the same. 'Come on, Jake... Look how cute he is!'

Jake, who had a severe lack in social skills, according to his parents and teachers, shook his head grumpily and sat back further in his chair. His body language spoke volumes. Austin pictured his sweet, bubbly Josiah as an older child. What lay ahead for him? Would he be a good father, handling their teenage years by himself?

Funny...just before he'd met Lucie again Belle

had got in his ear about setting up an online dating profile and he'd actually considered it. It was time he at least thought about opening himself up to the prospect of having *someone* in his life at some point in the future.

Not that he could think about that now, because...well, Lucie.

He pulled out the card game he'd brought with him, placing it on the table between them. 'I thought we'd try playing a game again,' he said.

Jake looked even more suspicious. But AJ had found interacting using a game sometimes shifted the focus in situations like this, and allowed his patients to open up more easily, with less intensity, so he could analyse their behaviour, symptoms, strengths and weaknesses. Last time, however, Jake had not played along.

This time, with his mother in the room, he seemed a little more willing, but it was still grunts and one-word answers when it came to his responses to AJ's questions. He did, however, keep glancing at Jetson, until Jetson seemed to get the message and laid a soft head on the boy's knee under the table.

'Hope you don't mind if I join you? Maple just got dropped off, by the way, AJ.'

They all turned as Lucie appeared in the doorway, with Maple. He knew she'd just finished an appointment down the hall. In fact, he'd asked her to join them afterwards if she was free. Maybe she would be able to help shed some light on how best to open Jake up, if he still didn't respond to him. She seemed to have a knack for bringing people out of themselves—especially his male patients. It was a feminine touch he certainly did not possess.

Jake's mother looked delighted as the second dog padded in. Jake just shrugged, but AJ didn't miss the way he was patting Jetson now, and how he'd welcomed Maple, too. The boy seemed a lot more relaxed as Lucie pulled up a chair, pondering the cards on the table.

She looked tired, but as well put together as ever. She was wearing navy fitted trousers and a matching jacket and a white blouse. Her hair was styled immaculately. She caught his eye, somehow sending him back to the fort the other day, in the twins' room, when he'd struggled not to kiss her.

'Your dog is beautiful,' Jake's mum enthused.

'Well, she's not exactly my dog,' Lucie replied, just as Maple snuffled her nose against Lucie's knee, eager for an invitation from her new temporary handler to prove herself at something useful. 'She'll be staying with AJ for a few days.'

'Looks like your dog to me.'

Lucie kept a straight face, but AJ didn't miss her glance of silent acquiescence. Maple was in his care, that was true, as he was helping Iris out, but Lucie clearly adored the dog. He caught her eye again, biting back a smile. Her being so close, so invested, did things to his insides—a certain kind of twisting and tangling that no one else had ever inspired in him. Not even Ebby.

Which was exactly his problem. That afternoon at the house, he'd wondered…what if she'd never left? What if he'd told her how he felt back then and she'd actually felt the same? Enough to have stayed? Maybe they'd have got serious…got married…

The guilt when he let his thoughts go down that road made him feel cold.

Helping John the way she had the other day… he would always be grateful she'd been there. So calm, collected, even when everyone else around them had panicked. It had just made him burn for her more, admire her more, wanting the best for her. She didn't speak about her dreams, but he knew she was still suffering just from seeing her tired eyes. That was why he wouldn't give up on convincing her to take on Maple while she was here. Maple would help her, he knew.

Not long after Lucie and Maple came in Jake had softened enough not only to answer his standard assessment questions, sneaked as usual into the act of playing the game, but to engross himself in a conversation Lucie started about his travel plans for the year.

It began when she told him, 'You look like the kind of boy who'd be on a swimming team or in a hiking group. Do either of those activities sound good to you?'

Jake's answers surprised him. Rather than being horrified when Lucie recounted how she'd once hiked up a mountain in flip-flops after a surprise tsunami in Thailand, he threw no end of questions at her, and seemed keen to explore the world, with friends, or maybe even solo 'like Bear Grylls'.

Not so closed off and reclusive as AJ had first assumed, then. In fact, thanks to Lucie's input and both dogs' calming presence, he now almost had enough to provide a diagnosis and a comprehensive treatment plan.

'Can I walk Jetson and Maple sometime?' Jake asked, on his way out.

AJ met his mother's eyes and felt both proud and relieved by the joy he saw in them.

'I think that can be arranged,' Lucie said.

But when she asked if they'd both be at the Paws Under the Stars event AJ was planning Lucie paused, and almost looked sad for a moment.

'I don't think so,' she replied cautiously. 'I'm just a locum here. I'll probably be gone by then.'

Austin's mood plummeted on the spot, and he averted his gaze, looking at Jetson, his tail wagging at the boy's enthusiastic goodbyes. In his head, he'd started to think she was always going to be here. The twins had asked if she would be. They were both talking about her more and more.

He would have to try harder not to let his work with her blend into their private lives, he decided, new resolve pounding through him. Even if that would be almost impossible in a village this size.

But when she asked if he wouldn't mind dropping her at her next home visit, seeing as her rental car was having some issues, he found himself agreeing, of course.

'Gramma May's feeling much better now,' Lucie told AJ, on the road towards Whitby. 'She told me to thank you and the twins for the flowers.'

'She thanked me herself, with a text message,' he replied, looking to the road ahead.

Lucie bit her lip as they sped past a road sign pointing to the ruined Gothic Whitby Abbey—Bram Stoker's inspiration for *Dracula*.

Of course she'd thanked him herself already, she thought. Gramma May was clearly a huge part of their lives, and every time she remembered how she'd asked her sweet, selfless grandma not to talk about AJ over the years she felt terrible. She'd apologised, of course, for asking Gramma to keep quiet about one of the people in the community she really cared about.

Gramma May had just said, 'It's fine. I understand.' Followed by something under her breath about how she knew she'd see the light eventually.

Lucie had left it there. Sometimes she had the distinct feeling that Gramma had long been rooting for her to come home and get together with Austin Johnstone, but Gramma May had never been one to talk about that kind of thing. And obviously there was no point stoking that fire. Had she not said just now that she'd be gone before the Spring Gala and the Paws Under the Stars event?

AJ hadn't even tried to change her mind.

'Want me to wait here with the dogs?' he asked her now, switching off the car engine.

She almost said yes, but her patient Constance was opening the door to her house already, and waving. Then she spotted the dogs.

Constance was bone-thin, dressed in a black shirt and a skirt that hung off her hips as she welcomed them all inside.

'I'm a huge dog fan—therapy dogs or otherwise,' she said, smiling, running her hands over Maple's soft ears as she ushered them through to the living room.

This was Lucie's first home visit to the fifty-seven-year-old, and immediately her appearance was striking alarm bells. She was pale, gaunt, hollow-cheeked, despite being so beautiful.

'I just don't know what's wrong, Doctor,' she explained with a sigh, sinking down into an olive-green sofa.'

A huge blown-up wedding photo obviously taken years ago took up almost all of one wall. The dogs took the space beside her on a chair, as if they owned the place.

She seemed to have trouble walking, Lucie noticed, and her every breath was long and drawn out. She wasn't eating well, Constance said, and she wasn't really able to exercise.

The dark circles around her eyes spoke of worry and sleepless nights—and, oh, Lucie knew that look well. It stared back at her from the mirror often enough. She probably looked exhausted herself right now, she thought, thanks to being up since three o'clock. Last night, in her dream, the water tank that had taken Jorge, took AJ too. The state she'd woken up in was almost unbearable to think about.

Her knee brushed AJ's as she sat on the other sofa. There was nowhere to move away from the friction. She could hardly have asked him to wait in the car after he'd driven her here, and after Constance had been so delighted by the dogs.

'I can't seem to use the bathroom properly,' Constance admitted now, somewhat bashfully. 'Nothing stays in me. It's almost like my body is rejecting food from all angles. And I'm just so tired all the time. Thanks for coming here… I'm not sure I could have made it to the surgery.'

AJ met Lucie's glance as she took the woman's blood pressure. She was just about to suggest a blood test, and request a stool sample, when Jetson started doing something strange.

'What's he doing?' Lucie asked AJ.

AJ stood up. He was trying not to show it, she could tell, but he looked deeply concerned. Jetson was rolling on the floor, over and over. He did it three times in a row before stopping and offering AJ his paw. AJ's eyes grew wide. He hadn't commanded the dog to do anything.

Constance stroked Maple's ears, watching in amusement, but the look on AJ's face had Lucie on edge. Something was going on…but what? Gosh, she was so tired.

He sat down again next to her and squeezed her knee. 'I need to talk to you outside,' he whispered.

Her heart bucked and leapt like a rabbit in her chest at the contact, and at the gravity of his tone. Constance was staring at them now. She nudged his hand away.

'My dear, you do look tired,' Constance commented suddenly.

Lucie shifted uncomfortably on the too-small seat. Rain had started pattering at the windows outside. 'Do I? I guess I didn't sleep much last night.'

'Nightmares again?' AJ probed.

Lucie nodded, defeated. Why lie?

'Constance, we should probably…'

Constance leaned towards her, put a feather-light hand over hers and cut her off. 'I know what that's like. My ex-husband haunts me…well, he did for years. Until I met my new one. That's him.' She bobbed her head at the wedding photo. 'That's why I made the photo so big. Cancels out the ex, somehow.'

Lucie huffed out a laugh.

But then Constance added, 'I don't see a ring on your finger. Is this man looking after you right?' A smile hovered on her pale lips. She looked between them where they sat on the tiny sofa.

'Lucie and I are just friends,' AJ explained bluntly, standing up again. He still looked distracted, and had started looking at something on his phone, bashing out a message.

'Nightmares about what, may I ask?' Constance looked interested.

'I was involved in an accident, of sorts, in Nepal,' she heard herself explaining, as she glanced at AJ. 'A building collapsed on my friend. I was too late to get him out...' She tailed off. Exhaustion was making her loose-lipped.

'But she saved other people, Constance. Children,' AJ said suddenly, shoving his phone back into his pocket and calling to Jetson.

Lucie frowned at him.

'Well, you did, Lucie,' he insisted. 'You went through more out there than most people can imagine. We're all proud of you. And you're going to be OK.'

Such conviction...

For a second, she didn't quite know what to say. She wanted to run to him, feel the comfort of his arms as well as his words. Thank goodness Constance was there. Lucie wasn't here to talk about what had happened to her—especially not in front of AJ. He'd been through enough on his own.

Maybe she was scared to talk about it for selfish reasons, she thought as she measured Constance's height and weight. In case she got addicted to his listening ear. It was just a countdown, really, till she was out of here—and she *was* going to leave.

'If you don't have a man, dear,' Constance went on, 'you should at least have a dog. I hear Maple will need a new foster home soon.'

Here we go.

Lucie packed up her things up Constance sang Maple's praises, saying how she'd have the dog herself if she didn't spend so much time at her daughter's place and the hospital.

Maple's big loving eyes seemed to plead with her. It was highly likely she was reading too much into this, but Maple did seem to have her own way of asking her if she'd be her new foster mum.

OK, yes, it was tempting. The benefits of a furry sidekick were clear: dogs were calming, funny, and a distraction from everyday woes. But it was already going to be hard enough leaving Gramma May, AJ and the twins.

Especially AJ…

There was absolutely no chance a live-in dog would be getting under her skin, too. Besides, she didn't need one. The nightmares would stop eventually. She would be OK.

'It's raining pretty hard now.'

AJ still looked troubled. She blinked, zipping up her bag, realising he'd been watching her.

'We should get going before it gets worse. The road back can be a nightmare at this hour...especially when it rains.'

CHAPTER TWELVE

THE SEAGULLS SQUAWKED a welcome to the Whitby seaside. The smell of fish and chips assaulted Austin's nose: the scent of their weekends as kids in this very place. Sure enough, the road home had been jammed, and because there were still a couple of hours before he needed to relieve Belle of the twins, who'd be doing homework anyway, they'd come here. The dogs needed to run.

'Are you sure you don't mind the beach?' he asked Lucie.

A gust of wind tugged at her fur-lined hood and blew her fringe back from her face. She squinted ahead.

'I don't mind a bit of rain.'

To her credit, she was not complaining, even though her immaculate look was being severely tested by the Yorkshire weather. He bit back a smile at the way she battled in vain with her hair the whole way from the seafront, down the steps and onto the vast yellow stretch of sand.

'Listen…' he said. Now that they had some open

space around them, he could process what had just happened. 'I might be getting ahead of myself, but I'm pretty sure Jetson just picked up on something with Constance.'

Lucie stopped, looked at him aghast. 'Cancer?'

'He gave me the signs,' he said into her wide-eyed gaze. He still couldn't quite believe it himself. 'I think you should…'

'Schedule a colonoscopy. I was thinking the same thing anyway,' she replied, shaking her head.

Austin's heart was racing. 'Lucie, if Jetson's right, we could have proof that the training works.'

She was still staring at him, seemingly lost in thought. 'I don't know what to say. That would be… Well, not great for Constance.'

'So we move fast. Push the tests through. She can get the help she needs as quickly as possible.'

The dogs sprinted ahead towards the surf, tails wagging in joy, and they watched them. He hoped he hadn't stepped on her toes, but this was everything he'd hoped Jetson would be able to do and more. His heart thrummed with adrenaline as he told her more about the signals Jetson had learned so far in the cancer detection training, and he barely noticed the weather. Unlike Lucie, who was still battling with her hair.

'You've probably done more challenging things in worse conditions,' he said, changing the topic, gesturing to her hair.

Lucie grimaced. 'You don't want to be in the Himalayas in a cyclone.'

He waited for her to go on, but she didn't. She stopped walking, crouched down for a pebble.

'Thank you, for what you said earlier…about being proud of me,' she told him suddenly, down on her haunches.

His stomach vaulted. He'd worried he'd sounded patronising—especially in front of Constance. 'I am proud of you,' he said stiltedly. 'The patients adore you…the dogs adore you.'

He stopped short of saying he adored her, too. There were too many ghosts in the wind who might judge him more than he could ever judge himself for the way he'd been feeling around her lately. And she'd moved his hand off her knee a little too fast back there. Almost as if she was afraid to show just how much his touch affected her. Maybe he *hadn't* been imagining something between them the other day, as they'd sat shoulder to shoulder in the kids' fort. Although he knew he wasn't imagining Lucie's insistence on leaving when her time here was up.

'I'm getting a lot out of spending all this time with…with the dogs.' She pressed her lips together, scanning his eyes. He knew she meant with *him*, as well as the dogs, but she wasn't going to say it. That was probably for the best. Because she wasn't going to stay here…

The twins were going to be gutted when she left.

The sea air was colder than he'd anticipated as they walked along the sand, but at least the rain had turned down a notch. Lucie hugged herself, her eyes on Maple. Should he bring up again the fact that she could take Maple home if she wanted, or would that be pushing it? The dog would at least be a good companion for the next few weeks if she woke up in the night.

'So, have you ever dated anyone, since Ebby?' she asked him now, stopping him in his tracks where the escarpment of the layered sea wall provided a sought-after sunbathing spot in the summer.

He faltered. He hadn't been expecting that. 'Um…no,' he admitted.

'You've never wanted to?'

He studied her, wondering how best to reply—and why she was even asking. He could admit that, yes, he wanted to now that she was here, but he wasn't going to admit that when she'd literally just reminded him, that morning, that she wouldn't even be here long enough to see the Spring Gala.

'Forget I said anything,' she muttered, clicking her tongue when he didn't reply.

The jagged rocks seemed an appropriate leaning post—uncomfortable, like the situation. He tossed a stone. Together they watched the seagulls swirling and squawking over the craggy cliffs ahead. She'd been chipping away at him bit by bit, whether she knew it or not, and now here he was, having to face a landslide.

'I feel bad that I think about Ebby less when I'm with you, Lucie.'

There. He'd said it.

Cold, spiderlike fingers scuttled up and down his spine as she turned to him. The dogs were specks in the distance, up towards the headlands, and he'd have done anything for their speed and agility, their ability to run a mile in a heartbeat—away from *this*.

'She was the mother of my children.'

Lucie pressed her back to the craggy wall beside him. 'I don't mean any disrespect. You know that... You know me. You and I are just friends. I know you loved her in a very different way...'

Austin's jaw clenched. She had no idea. 'What do *you* know? I'm betraying her memory right now.'

She pushed away from the wall and faced him, her hair blowing in tendrils around her face. 'We're not doing anything, AJ.'

'But I want to.' The words were torn from somewhere deep inside him.

Lucie sucked in a breath but she didn't move, didn't speak. Her eyes were full of questions, fear, trepidation...desire?

Then she said. 'Why now, AJ?' Her voice was so soft her words were almost imperceptible.

'I never did kiss you properly back then,' he

said, stepping closer, his own fierce longing for her propelling him further than his common sense should've allowed.

Lucie swallowed, frowning through her fringe. 'I didn't think you wanted to.'

'Did *you* want me to?' he tested, finding her eyes in her whirling hair.

For a long moment, her gaze roved over his mouth.

'Tell me, Luce. Was there ever a moment, before you left, that you thought about it? Even for one second?'

Her eyes flooded with emotion—right before she squeezed them shut.

He could have kissed her. She'd have been putty in his hands—he could just tell. Suddenly he could see, as if someone had ripped the blinkers off him. She'd looked at him like this before, when she'd seen him making out with Tina…or had it been Sasha…at his seventeenth birthday party.

'Well?' he pressed. He needed to hear her say it.

'No. We were only ever friends, AJ,' she said. 'Like we are now.'

He bit down hard on his cheek. So that was how she wanted to play it.

Tearing his eyes away, he carried on up the beach. He shouldn't have said anything. Stupid… *stupid*.

'AJ,' she said, hurrying after him. 'I didn't mean for this to get complicated for you. I know we're getting all tied up together, because of the dogs and everything, but if I take Maple we can make the rounds separately...'

'Don't be ridiculous!'

He spun around. That was out of the question—especially now Jetson had picked up on something with Constance.

'I mean, yes, you can take Maple. Great idea. But how do you *really* feel, Lucie? This isn't just about protecting me from *complications*!'

Lucie's gaze froze on his. The dogs sprinted back to them, circling them, asking to play. For once, they both ignored them.

'Isn't it getting complicated for you, too?' he said. 'Seeing everything that's changed? Building something here for yourself again?'

'Of *course* it is.' Her eyes clouded over.

He cupped her face, impulsively drawing her closer with one hand, forcing her eyes to his. She pressed her cheek into his palm.

'Do you like being friends with me, Lucie? Tell me the truth.'

The longest, most agonised breath escaped her flaring nostrils. '*You* wanted to be friends.'

'That wasn't my question.'

The warmth of her seeped into him. Her lips parted temptingly...an invitation. He leaned closer, dragged a thumb along her lower lip.

Looking up at him again through lowered

lashes, she whispered, 'You were only ever my best friend.'

'Yes. I was. Do you like making *friends* like me and then running away into disaster zones? Does it make you happy? Because you don't seem happy.'

'That's not fair, AJ.'

Her lips brushed over the skin of his palm as she spoke, shooting blood straight to his groin.

'I'll get better—you said it yourself. And my work makes me happy. I *want* to get back to working overseas. It's where I belong.'

Uncertainty flickered in her eyes—just the briefest flash—and he tucked the silent insight away in his mind, dropping his hand from her face. 'You keep telling yourself that.'

'I love my work,' she asserted, squaring her shoulders. 'And I'd love it if we could be friends without all...*this*.' She wiggled her hand between them, as if shooing some kind of annoying pest away.

A slow boil started in his blood, but he kept his face neutral as he turned back the way they'd come. He changed the subject to the dogs, and of course she went with it. No point talking about anything that actually meant anything—not when it sparked the need either to kiss or fight.

At least they were on the same page. Wanting someone else was confusing as hell, but *this* was exactly why he wouldn't do *anything* with Lucie

Henderson—even if she admitted she wanted to… which she clearly was not going to do.

This need she seemed to have to prove herself—hadn't she proved enough? What she did was meaningful, but what about her *own* mental health? No one could do the kind of work she did for ever and not be affected…for ever. And now he'd just picture her out there, her beautiful mind and body dancing with all that danger, *another* woman he couldn't keep from being claimed by something out of his control.

Let it go, Austin.

She was going back to it, whatever he did or said. That was just what Lucie did. His heart didn't need this torture and neither did his children. They'd been through enough.

If only every inch of his body and soul didn't still burn to protect her. Like it had when he'd first caught her crying as a helpless little kid.

CHAPTER THIRTEEN

LUCIE FORCED HERSELF AWAKE. Sitting up in bed, she felt the sweat slide down her back, sticking her shirt to her skin. Three a.m. It was always three a.m. now.

Oh, God.

The rumbling aftershock in her dream… Jorge's face melting like butter into AJ's. Jorge had become AJ stuck between trembling walls, broken glass and twisted steel.

'Run!' he'd yelled at her loudly, his face distorted in panic.

But she'd grabbed him and pressed herself hard against him, holding on tightly. Moving hadn't even been an option. She wasn't letting go of him…wasn't going anywhere.

Then the wall tumbled down on both of them.

Lucie fumbled for her water, letting the huge glugs wet her parched throat. Her breath still hadn't quite found her when Maple padded in. The Retriever leapt onto the bed, dropped to her side and pressed a soft, furry face to her belly through the duvet.

I'm here, she seemed to say.

Lucie stroked her soft fur, seeking solace in the steady warmth of the dog's presence. Her big brown eyes gleamed with a certain knowledge in the faint light from the hall.

Calm, Maple seemed to say. *Relax, I'm here. You've got this.*

Lucie's breathing slowed. She closed her eyes again, allowing herself to drift, her hand still locked in Maple's fur, the rhythm of the dog's breathing a soothing lullaby.

Maple didn't move for the rest of the night. And Lucie didn't wake till nine-thirty a.m.

'You look well rested,' Gramma May observed when she wandered into the kitchen, dazed by the morning light streaming through the windows. Usually it was still dark when she dragged herself out of her nightmares and down the stairs.

'I feel rested,' she admitted, reaching for the coffee.

But the dream was still fresh in her mind's eye. Why did Jorge always turn into AJ now?

He was getting under her skin as she'd known he would.

And the conversation on the beach had hardly helped… The look in his eyes when he'd said, *'I feel bad that I think about Ebby less when I'm with you, Lucie.'*

He'd finally opened the door to at least discussing what might have happened between them back then, and she'd slammed it shut in his face. But what was she supposed to say? She was leaving again soon, and he felt bad enough already for liking her…maybe for liking her before he'd even met Ebby?

She'd humiliated him, probably, by pushing him away. But he had no idea that even now she could still hear Claire laughing with him, teasing him about how 'little lost Lucie' followed him around like a puppy dog. She could still hear the silence that had followed from him. It was why she'd run right out of his life. Why hadn't he defended her? She'd always figured he'd been too busy eyeing up Claire, who'd been 'showing him things' that Lucie couldn't. Now, no matter what he said or how he looked at her, it was too late for them.

The doorbell rang. Maple barked.

Oh, no…

'Gramma, wait!'

But Gramma May was already heading for the door. Lucie barely had time to belt up her dressing gown before AJ was stepping into the kitchen, all six foot of him, bringing with him the leafy fresh air and a spicy waft of cologne.

Jetson padded in behind him and greeted Maple with a bum-sniff.

'Did you only just wake up?' He suppressed a

smile as she struggled to separate him from the version of AJ she'd clung to in her dream.

God, did she have pillow creases across her cheeks? She let her hair hide her face.

'I thought I told you I have the rental car back?' She gestured to it through the window, parked outside on the street. 'You don't have to drive me anywhere today.'

He stared her down, and the lump in her throat grew golf-ball-sized. They'd both made things a little awkward yesterday. Well, OK, *she'd* made it worse by going into denial mode.

'I thought I'd give you this,' he said, pressing a stack of papers down on the table. 'It's the research I have so far…what I've gathered from the dogs involved in cancer detection.'

'Oh…' She pulled her gown around her tighter. 'Thanks. I've pushed for Constance's colonoscopy this afternoon.'

'Good,' he said.

Then he frowned at her, as if he was seeing straight through her robe. She still couldn't get yesterday out of her head…the way his eyes had burned into hers on the beach.

'I can wait while you get dressed,' he said now.

She blinked at him.

'You wanted to see Samuel get his new therapy dog? He's obsessed with Maple, too.'

'That's the boy in hospital with severe diabetes, right?' she said, looking around for her phone.

His attention on her made her knees as weak as her resolve as she swept past him. How could she ever forget the intensity in his eyes when he'd asked: *'Do you like being friends with me, Lucie? Tell me the truth.'*

Gramma May pulled a coffee cup out for him and patted his head affectionately as she put it down. He beamed up at her. 'Glad you're feeling better, Gramma May,' he said, helping himself to coffee and a biscuit from a plate on the table.

'I'm better now that Lucie's doing better,' she replied. 'She slept so well with Maple last night. I'm guessing that was your idea, Austin?'

'Both of us had the idea,' Lucie corrected, lifting up a pile of magazines. 'But it's only for a few days, till we can find another foster home for Maple. Honestly...where *is* my phone?'

'Lucie.' Austin's tone caught her off guard. He grabbed her phone up from the counter by the kettle and strode to her, holding it out of her reach when she tried to take it.

'What's wrong? Tell me.' He was whispering, although suddenly it was only them in the room.

'I had another dream,' she said. Well, that was half of the reason why she was so flustered in his presence. 'It wasn't as awful once Maple came in, but...'

'So she's helping you already?'

He smiled, and she almost melted. He looked so hot in his leather jacket, and those jeans made his bum look pert and perfect. But that was not for her to contemplate. She'd done the right thing, throwing him off the scent about her real feelings.

'You don't have to do all this with Maple,' he whispered to her now, his back still to Gramma May. 'If it's too much I can take Maple back. I can—'

'No,' she said to his muscular chest as he shielded her from the room. 'I want to do this.'

A moment passed, then he nodded, scanning her face thoughtfully.

The voice in her head was taunting her. *You are the last thing he needs. He's just distracted because he's been single for so long. Stay away...*

'But I told you. I don't want to make things difficult for you.'

His jaw clenched and regret dashed through his eyes. 'About what I said yesterday,' he told her, keeping his voice low. 'I was out of line. You were right. We *should* try to be...'

He stopped short of saying it. But it hovered in the space between their lips.

Friends.

A current of hot white energy bolted through her veins at his steadfast gaze. Maybe he *had* felt something for her back then...back before she tore everything apart.

No, Lucie. He's just confused. Because you're here now and he hasn't dated anyone since Ebby!

'What are you two whispering about?' Gramma

May looked just a little bit amused as she rolled her eyes.

'Give me ten minutes,' Lucie said, taking the phone from his hands and hurrying upstairs.

Whatever was going on, the least she could do was show up for Thera Pups—the second most important thing in the world for AJ aside from the twins. The funny thing was, it was starting to mean just as much to her, too.

Lucie's ten-year-old insulin-dependent diabetic patient Samuel had been in and out of the surgery and the hospital since Lucie's arrival in the village, following several scary episodes of unconsciousness—one of them happening at school. It had freaked out a lot of the other kids and left him feeling a deep sense of shame, along with terror that it might happen again.

He wasn't doing so well when they reached the hospital.

'We've had some setbacks,' a student nurse whispered on their way in. 'That last attack really shook him up. I explained that's why you've kept him in, Dr Henderson, but he wants to go home.'

'Is that right?' AJ asked the boy, taking over as the nurse left them to it. 'Is it the jelly they're feeding you?' he whispered, moving the IV aside so he could take his seat beside the boy.

Samuel's mouth twitched. 'No, that's the best part. Even though it's sugar-free.'

'Do they have strawberry flavour?' Lucie followed up. 'That's Maple's favourite.'

'Dogs don't eat jelly!'

Using the hand command she'd learned from AJ, she directed Maple to place her two front paws on the bed by Samuel's head, and without further command the dog obliged, and graced his cheek with a lick for good measure.

'That's her way of telling you you're right and I was wrong,' Lucie said. 'But who knows what your *own* dog will like eating, huh?'

She threw AJ a conspiratorial look.

The little boy frowned. 'I don't have a dog of my own.'

'Well…you *didn't* have a dog,' AJ said, signalling to the nurse standing by the door. 'But Dr Henderson and I were kind of hoping you might like to look after Bingo?'

The door opened.

Samuel's squeal almost deafened them.

One of the ladies Lucie had met that time at the farm walked in, with a cream and brown beagle on a blue lead. She watched Maple do a ballet dancer spin on the floor by way of greeting Bingo, and couldn't help laughing. Gosh, this dog was a star. So beautiful…almost a mind-reader, too. Maybe Maple could take the disease detection training too, she found herself thinking. Like this beagle had.

'Bingo is a very special dog,' AJ said now, running a hand over the dog's long, floppy ears. 'He's specially trained to help people like you who have diabetes. He knows hown to alert you when your blood sugar level is dropping or spiking.'

Samuel's eyes widened. He hugged the dog close, obviously attached already.

'These dogs undergo extensive training to be able to do what they do,' Lucie said, feeling AJ's eyes dart to her.

She'd read everything he'd written over the past week. It was fascinating.

Samuel's mother poked her head in and took a seat as Lucie continued.

'He can detect isoprene—that's a common natural chemical found in human breath. It increases, the lower your blood sugar is—'

'So, keep Bingo close,' AJ cut in.

The new dog had been placed on the bed now, and was licking Samuel's face.

Samuel's mother was wiping tears of joy from her face. 'I can't thank you and Thera Pups enough, Dr Johnstone.'

When Lucie looked up again, AJ was smiling at her, and her blood raced, remembering how she'd clung to him in her dream. This felt so good, she'd almost forgotten how at odds they were.

Clamming up on him yesterday hadn't been her finest moment. Pretending she felt nothing? So selfish! The truth was, she'd panicked. What if she let him in, let herself fall the way she'd always wanted to with him, and *then* he said he wasn't ready after all? Or that he needed more for his son and daughter than some itchy-footed traveller with no real roots and no history of settling down?

You still have no intention of settling down, she reminded herself.

Although it *was* getting tiring, moving around all the time, always trying to outrun the next disaster...

'What do you think, Lucie?'

'Huh?' She'd zoned out, her eyes on AJ...thinking about AJ. Again.

'Should I bring Bingo to Paws Under the Stars?' Samuel asked hopefully. 'I can dress him up...'

'If you're well enough,' AJ said gently. He turned to Lucie. 'We're organising a little outing for several kids who've spent time on the ward this year the night of the event.'

'I want to see them in their costumes, with all the lights!' Samuel grinned, stroking a hand across Bingo's soft head and receiving another lick in response.

He looked delighted at the prospect, and Lucie smiled as AJ's phone rang. She watched him step into the hall with it. It was awe-inspiring, how much AJ's organisation was helping people heal, each one in a different way, all because of these dogs.

'I want to see them in their costumes too,' Lucie heard herself say, before she could even remind herself that she wouldn't be around for it. She'd be somewhere else by then…somewhere far away.

AJ was back. The look on his face made her adrenaline spike. Something was up.

She threw him a questioning look. He shook his head.

'Do you mind taking the dogs?' he asked her. 'Something's come up. I'll catch up with you in an hour or so if I can.' He paused, lowered his voice. 'And if I can't, call me when you know Constance's colonoscopy results?'

Her mind swam. 'I will. Is it the twins?'

'Yes, but they're OK… I think.

AJ looked frazzled. With a quick goodbye to Samuel, he darted back towards the door.

CHAPTER FOURTEEN

'DAD, WE NEED more tissues!'

Austin suppressed a harried sigh from the kitchen, where he'd just realised they were out of canned food. Belle wasn't exactly responsible for keeping the cupboards stocked, but she'd used to do it anyway. Now, with all her wedding planning, she was spending more time away. He was gradually having to do more and more to keep the big house in order. Which was, as it emerged, quite a lot for one person.

'You're doing OK now, Austin. You've got this!'

He repeated his sister's words in his head, trying to believe they were true.

'Dad, can I have some hot chocolate?'

'Um… I'm not sure that's what you should be having. Chocolate doesn't cure colds, guys.'

'Yes, it definitely does,' Ruby insisted from the other room.

Ruby and Josiah were both sick. They had the same bug that was striking everyone down lately. After the school had called, and he'd left the hospital to collect them, he'd bundled the two sniffling children up, deposited them on the couch with a cartoon show, and tried to ignore the mountain of work he was supposed to be doing.

The kids came first, but what was he supposed to feed them now? He scanned the pantry. Nothing of use but some pasta, and there wasn't any sauce. They couldn't exactly live on hot chocolate.

Or could they?

The doorbell irritated him, but he forced his face into some semblance of calm as he opened it.

'Hi,' Lucie said. 'Am I interrupting?'

He blinked, looking over her shoulder for the dogs. She'd texted to say she'd take them home, and he'd been too distracted to reply with anything other than a thumbs-up emoji.

'They're with Gramma May,' she explained, reading his mind. 'They're fine. She'll look after them for as long as we need. She asked me to bring you this.'

Lucie held out a Tupperware box and he grinned. Wafts of deliciousness sang to his nose and his stomach grumbled.

'That woman is a godsend,' he groaned, standing aside to let her in.

'I also brought you these. I dare you to make one last all day.' She held out a tiny box of chocolates from Cynthia's shop and he took them, touched. He'd used to buy one for her at a time and dare her the same thing.

She remembered that?

Minutes later, Lucie was ladling steaming soup into bowls, which she had somehow located herself, along with spoons, while he bashed out an email to a client that he'd been meaning to write for hours. She took two bowls to the twins, who accepted them gleefully and asked her to fetch some more tissues—which she did, without complaint.

Sending the email, he sat back in his chair, the warmth of his own bowl of soup already calming him.

'Anything else I can do?' she enquired. 'I noticed your cupboards are bare.'

She folded her arms, leaned back on the counter.

Why was she being so nice? He'd pretty much abandoned her back at the hospital, with no explanation. Of course one of the school staff would have told someone, who'd have told someone else about the twins—which was no doubt how Gramma May had found out in time to make them soup. Everyone knew everything around here.

He ran a hand across his head. Would it be wrong to ask Lucie to get some groceries? He had so much work to do, and he'd already cancelled two clients today.

But she was already grabbing the shopping bag from the hook by the door. 'Don't worry,' she said gently. 'I can see you're busy. Take some time for yourself, AJ. Enjoy the chocolates.'

'I already have,' he admitted, and she snorted.

'I knew you wouldn't make them last!'

He'd been so in love with her laugh. One time when he'd caught her crying, he'd attempted his first cartwheel just to make her laugh. Three hours later he'd been laid up in A&E with a sprained wrist.

Thrown now, he fought the urge to refuse her help. She shouldn't have come here, really. His kids were sick. It was his issue to deal with, not hers. Lucie didn't need to be involved.

Not when they'd end up liking her even more than they did already. And not when he might, too.

'Lucie, come and watch this bit!' Josiah called out. 'It's so funny!'

'We can rewind it later,' she called back. 'Try not to laugh too much without me.'

'Can we have hot chocolate when you get back?' Ruby called out. 'Dad says it will cure us.'

'I did not say that!' Austin said.

With a squeeze of his shoulder, Lucie made her exit, and he listened to the door shut behind her, the crunch of her feet on the gravel driveway. This was what a community did. But Lucie wasn't really a part of it. He'd assumed she didn't want to be. Maybe she was warming to the way things were around here? Perhaps a little trip down memory lane was getting her nostalgic?

It was all just a bit weird, though, especially after what had happened on the beach. He'd given her every chance to confess she might have liked him too, back then, and to admit that she might want more now, but she'd brushed him off.

Maybe this was her way of trying to get their friendship back on track?

He should probably just accept it, he thought. He'd done enough to make things awkward.

An hour passed. Then another one. He managed to straighten out the house, send more emails, and rearrange his schedule in case the twins were sick for a few more days. His heart thudded wildly as he found himself removing the paperwork from the estate agents from the sideboard drawer and studying his house valuation for the thousandth time.

Stop assuming Belle will always be here when you know the clock is ticking, he told himself. *All this space will be too much.*

Still, when it came to calling the estate agent, he couldn't do it.

And Lucie wouldn't leave his head.

He'd told himself to keep away from her—had left her this morning without involving her, short of leaving both dogs in her care. But here she was again. And here he was…letting her in.

This had to change, he decided, abandoning the paperwork on the kitchen table and sighing. When she got back here with the shopping he'd insist she go straight home and not come back.

'I got the results of Constance's colonoscopy!'

Lucie burst past him with bulging bags of shopping the second he opened the door. She dropped them to the counter so hard that three oranges rolled out, and then turned to him, holding out her phone.

'AJ, Jetson was right. Look.'

Mind reeling, he took the phone from her, studied the report and scans.

'The tumour is tiny…in the lining of the bowel. Treatable with surgery, of course. It hasn't spread…' She tailed off.

He didn't know what to say. She didn't give him the chance to speak—she just threw her arms around him.

He hugged her back, stunned into silence, still trying to get his head around the news. Jetson had picked up on this cancer before they had. This was huge. They could analyse the chemical compounds in the cancer he'd sniffed out and put another piece of the puzzle together.

'This is massive, AJ.' Lucie still held his shoulders, elated. 'Your dog is so smart. And you are amazing for training him.'

Her eyes were shining with pride and awe and, caught in the moment, he almost kissed her. Almost.

Quickly, he stepped back—just as she did the same, flushing.

He helped her unpack the shopping, discussing with her what this meant for Constance, for his research. They were both so excited he almost forgot that things had been so tense between them before.

Four hours later, Lucie was still there. She and the kids were deep into a programme on the mysteries of Ancient Egypt—Josiah's new fascination—and Ruby had painted Lucie's nails. If it wasn't for the occasional sneeze and foghorn blow into a tissue, he might have assumed no one was sick at all...

'Daddy, can Lucie sleep over?' Ruby asked from the sofa cushions, where she was huddled against Lucie. Josiah, on her other side, was lost in a book.

Lucie bit back a smile. 'I don't think so, sweetie. You need to get better.'

'And you don't want to make Lucie sick too, do you?' Austin followed up from the adjacent armchair, even while his chest hollowed out.

It was late already—gone seven p.m.—but the twins were clinging on to Lucie like glue, and he had been able to do a few things around the house that he'd been planning to do, thanks to her looking out for them.

If he was planning to sell the house he'd have a lot *more* to do, he thought as his insides twisted.

When Josiah started yawning he stood, ordering them both up the stairs. They protested, of course, but Lucie offered to read from his favourite book about Egypt.

Austin shot her a questioning look as he scooped Ruby up in his arms, and she shrugged. 'I like

Egypt,' she offered. 'I got stuck in a pyramid once, in Cairo. They almost closed it up with me inside it…like a mummy.'

'Are you going to be *our* mummy?' Ruby interjected sleepily.

Austin froze. Lucie's face flushed red.

'That's not what she meant, honey,' he said quickly, motioning Josiah to follow him up the stairs—but not before catching the look in Lucie's eyes. There it was: a hint of sadness and confusion where he'd expected to see laughter.

What did she really want? Certainly not to be anyone's mummy—although she'd make a better one than she thought she would, judging by how she'd been acting around the twins. But she couldn't give up the thrill of running round disaster zones, surely.

Lucie followed close behind Josiah, letting him lead. She was quiet while he got the kids changed, fetched them more tissues, and glasses of water in case they got dry throats in the night. He perched on the edge of Josiah's bed while Lucie took a chair and read from the book between their beds. The soft lull of her voice almost sent him to sleep, too.

He studied Lucie's profile in the night light and shadows. He was a ship on a rocky ocean…sailing right into a sinkhole opening up in the seabed. Her being here now was great, but it wouldn't feel great when he was forced to miss her again. Another woman gone in a flash, almost as fast as she'd arrived.

'Are you going to be our mummy?'

The kids craved a mother figure in their life—especially Ruby. Belle could only do so much, he thought. But this little unit of three he was cultivating alone would be a lot for any woman to take on. Especially a woman with one foot already out through the door, like Lucie...

'Let me get you that box before you go,' he said pointedly when they were back downstairs.

She followed him into the kitchen and stayed quiet while he washed and dried Gramma May's Tupperware. Too quiet. It made him feel nervous, as if the walls were closing in, trying to force them together when she should leave without the twins begging her not to go.

He turned around. She was looking at him, holding the house valuation papers in her hands. His stomach plummeted into his shoes.

'You're selling the house?' she said, her voice thick and unsteady.

'I don't know... Maybe.'

Dropping to a chair at the table, she stared at him, then at the papers, as if trying to convince herself it was real.

He took the seat opposite. 'I think I have to,' he explained. 'Belle's moving in with her fiancé, soon to be husband, shortly...'

'But this house has been in your family for years! Generations!'

'Well…' He struggled for the right thing to say. The truth was the truth. 'I can't manage all this on my own, Luce. It's too big for just the three of us.'

Lucie drummed her nails on the table, looking between him and the paperwork. 'I understand. But, honestly, I don't know what I'm feeling about this. I know I don't actually have any right to feel anything.'

'Of course you do,' he said, as the hurt on her face tore at him. 'You practically grew up here with me.'

He bit hard on his cheeks. He and Ebby had never lived here together, but he and Lucie… Well, Lucie had used to walk in here just as if it was her own house, without even ringing the bell!

Lucie blew air through her lips. She wasn't wearing as much make-up today. It made her eyes seem lighter, her skin paler. She looked younger—more like the girl who'd turned his life upside down by leaving with no explanation at all.

She still hadn't really given him a good reason for that—she'd said she hadn't wanted to miss him, or anyone here? It didn't make sense… But she hated him dragging it up and he didn't particularly want to antagonise her.

He found her hand on the table, as if he might comfort her for stomping on some precious part of her own past. She let him this time, just for a second, before standing up and facing him, folding her arms again.

Her shoulders were tight and he waited. Whatever she was about to say was going to be important. He braced himself—but a sudden flash of lightning cut her off. She shot to the window as the thunder crashed in quick succession, groaning as the rain that had been a light drizzle all afternoon turned into a thunderous shower, the strength of which could probably cause whiplash.

'Are you kidding me? This has got to be the wettest spring on record,' he said, walking up behind her.

She was inches from his face. Her eyes bored into his like a drill through to his brain, and he stopped short of asking if she was still going to walk home.

Of course she shouldn't walk home in this, Austin. You're supposed to be a gentleman.

'It'll stop soon enough…come through to the lounge. I'm sure there's an episode or two that you haven't seen about Ancient Egypt,' he offered, and though she looked conflicted, she agreed.

A cloud of white-hot tension popped straight back into the room and followed them both to the sofa.

CHAPTER FIFTEEN

THE AFTERSHOCK WAS almost as bad as the earthquake—only this time Lucie was at ground zero. Gripping the doorframe, she struggled for breath as the dust gripped her throat in a choke-hold. Jorge had ushered the kids towards her, but now he was turning back, looking for something.

'Where are you going?'

'She wants her backpack…there's a photo of her mother in it! She's lost her mother, Lucie.'

'It's too dangerous, Jorge. Come with us.'

'Take them outside. I'll only be two seconds.'

The kids were screaming, crying in terror. They came first—that was the agreement. The kids came first.

Dread pooled in her stomach. They were in a tiny village school halfway up a mountain road that had already been semi blocked by fallen trees. It had taken ages just to get there.

'Jorge, it's not safe!'

No sooner had the words left her mouth than

another tremor shook the ground so hard that they were all thrown sideways.

Somehow she'd made it to the door with the kids, pushing them through into the open. *'Go! Go!'*

Behind her, Jorge screamed an agonising scream as a steel cabinet crashed down across his leg, trapping him.

'Jorge, no!'

She hurried back, shoved it with all her strength, but it wasn't budging. It would have fallen on the kids if she hadn't got them out.

He was gasping for breath. Blood rushed through his jeans below the knee.

'You're going to be OK,' she soothed as the red stickiness seeped ominously through his clothing.

The blood was all over her as she locked her hands under his shoulders and tried to hoist him up. He wouldn't move. He was well and truly stuck.

'Go! Just go, Lucie!'

'No, I'm not leaving you!'

The light fixtures swung overhead. A chilling, creaking sound froze her to the bone. It was happening again. She stood there, torn, as the walls began to crumble and she was blinded by yet more dust. Jorge had gone eerily silent. Lucie fought the giant sob welling in her throat—right before the thousand-gallon water tank crashed down from its steel perch, smothering him completely.

'No! Jorge, no! No...'

'Lucie! Lucie, wake up!'

AJ's voice dragged her from the dream. She started awake, hot, sweating.

'What? What happened?'

AJ was crouched on the carpet beside the sofa, his shirt open, unbuttoned, as if he'd pulled it on in a hurry. A blanket that must have fallen off her lay crumpled by his knees.

'You fell asleep...you had a nightmare. God, is this what happens to you every time you have one of these dreams?'

He pressed a cool hand to her cheek and she sucked in a breath, scrambling to sit up.

'I'm so sorry.' She blinked beneath her fringe. 'How loudly did I scream? Did I wake the twins?'

'They're fine...' He frowned, moving beside her on the cushions, urging her against his shoulder.

She slumped against him, defenceless, comforted by the bulk and naked warmth of his exposed chest. It lasted hardly any time at all before his unexpected presence caused all her other emotions to pile up and spill out. Her arms snaked around him impulsively, her hands clutching fistfuls of his hair and open shirt as she cried.

'I had no idea,' he growled, rubbing her shoulder, smoothing her hair back.

Relief had her sobbing like she'd never sobbed before. She'd never let it out. She'd bottled it up. Too afraid of her dreams getting worse if she uncorked all those emotions. But AJ was here. He was here, and she felt better already, with each sob into his chest. She could let it all out into him—he would take it and keep her safe, like he always had. It felt so good, finally, to be safe in his arms again.

Eventually, embarrassed, she pulled her head away, pressed the heels of her palms to her eyes. Not only had she passed out from exhaustion on his sofa, in front of the TV, she'd gone and shown him how deeply messed up she was.

'What you must have seen...' he said gruffly.

When she turned he was looking at her in fierce defiance. He looked angry, for what she'd been through, and sleepy too. Had she drawn him downstairs with her screams? It was bad enough that he'd left her here instead of waking her up.

'Why didn't you wake me up when I first dropped off?'

'It was raining, and you needed sleep! I told Gramma May you were safe, don't worry.'

He swept stray strands of damp hair back behind her ears and drew a thumb across her cheek. She wanted to sink deeper into him, into the comfort. The look in his eyes was undoing her again. Just like it had on the beach.

'I should go,' she managed.

But she was still shaking. Her legs would have buckled beneath her if she hadn't already been sitting down.

'You don't have to go anywhere,' he said gently.

'You have enough to deal with. What if the twins wake up feeling sick? I don't want to cause any trouble.'

'Lucie—damn it, just stop. You're not causing me any trouble. They're fast asleep.'

AJ fetched her a glass of water. He ran his hand up and down her back as she drank it and she realised she was still trembling, both with adrenaline and humiliation.

'Did I…did I shout your name?' she asked weakly, wiping at her face.

'*My* name?' He frowned.

She hid her eyes from him behind her hair.

Great, why not drop yourself in it a bit more, Lucie?

'Why would you have shouted *my* name? You don't dream of *me* in a landslide, or a hurricane, or whatever else you're trying to get away from in these nightmares, do you?'

She closed her eyes, breathed deep and hard. 'Sometimes my dreams get crazy, if you can believe that.'

'Can you talk to me about it?' he asked, pulling the blanket back up around her.

She stared at it, at his familiar eyes. It wasn't exactly what she'd come here to do. But his eyes were so kind, and his mouth was set in *I'll listen but won't speak* mode. Trusting him was second nature.

And so it all poured out of her. How she'd watched the water tank fall, how she'd had to escort the kids to the mountain road, willing herself to find strength as they wound around fallen debris to the sounds of distant screams. They'd gone there to talk with the kids, some of whom had lost parents, friends, siblings… Everything.

She told him how she'd had to direct the rescue team to where Jorge was buried and had watched him being carried out in a white body bag…how she'd made the call to his wife—the call no wife ever wanted to receive.

AJ must have suffered the same kind of shock, she realised. He would have heard the same gut-wrenching sobs coming from himself after finding out Ebby was gone. She shouldn't be telling him all this, she thought in dismay.

But he wasn't making it about him. And AJ's arm around her shoulders was the steady kind of certainty she hadn't felt in years.

The way he listened without comment or judgement made her tell him more. Jorge had had two kids, an expat wife in Cusco who'd moved there for him, built a life with him. It should've been *Lucie* who had died in the Kathmandu Valley that day, not him. It wasn't as if *she* had any significant others…no kids, not even any parents left.

'I should never have taken him there!'

AJ held her closer, as if he knew he was holding her together. And just as her heart rate started to calm he said, 'Don't go back to that job, Lucie. I'm begging you.'

Oh, God.

Patting her eyes, she struggled to regain her composure.

But he wasn't done. 'Even if you *can* go back to that kind of placement, Lucie, do you even want to? Surely there's a limit to how much one person can take?'

She shook her head. 'I need to go out there again. I promised myself I would carry on doing what Jorge can't...'

'Lucie...' He swivelled her round to face him. His face had that same look she'd seen on the beach: the serious AJ.

'I don't know what else I would do if I didn't go back.'

'You could stay here...in Brookborough.'

He held her stare. How was it possible for him to convey so much emotion with just a glance? she thought, leaning closer, suspended in the moment, magnetised. It was as if she could feel his soul now, and he could feel hers—as if every part of each of them was reaching out and connecting to the other. They were so close their breath mingled and the heat from his body radiated off him, calling to her. He wanted to kiss her. And she wanted the same...so badly...

No.

With difficulty, she pulled her hands back, drew the blanket tighter around her.

AJ stood, raked his hands through his hair.

'I can't stay in Brookborough, AJ.'

She'd promised herself she wouldn't let Jorge down. Besides, AJ knew she wasn't and could never be Ebby, or anything *like* the kind of woman he needed. She wasn't mother material, for a start! If she stayed, he'd figure that out soon enough.

Aunt Lina was back in her brain now. *'Kids are burdens,'* she'd always said. *'So are men, if you must know.'*

Lucie's teenage self had come to believe that. Lina was a successful, perpetually single woman who'd done everything by and for herself and thrived.

Her advice had always been, *'You can only rely on yourself in this life, Lucie!'*

Ostensibly she belonged nowhere, to no one, and that was working out just fine. Or had she just been telling herself that this whole time? In order to give Gramma space to live her retirement years in peace? To get away from being AJ's helpless little puppy dog shadow?

'You should try and get some sleep,' he said, cutting into her uncomfortable thoughts. 'I'll walk you home when the sun's up,' he said, coolly.

The moment was ruined.

To her dismay, he turned and made his way back up the stairs.

Lucie made sure to sneak out before the sun came up.

CHAPTER SIXTEEN

AUSTIN PULLED THE car into the sweeping drive-way of the Mayflower Care Home just outside Staithes. A flock of birds darted like arrows from the willow trees and Jetson's ears pointed sky-wards in the passenger seat. Being well-trained, he didn't try to run for any birds when Austin let him out of the car, but he wanted to. A feeling Austin knew well.

Heading for the entrance, he saw the late-after-noon sun send dapples across the white stone walls of the stately home turned care facility. In the dis-tance, boats formed tiny black dots on a molten golden sea. Was Lucie here yet?

They were meeting one of Lucie's patients to-gether. It would be the first time they'd been to-gether since their discussion at his house. Lucie had called him, said she needed him and Jetson for this one. Her invitation had come as a bit of a surprise, as she'd taken to going it alone with Maple lately.

He'd shot her brief texts from time to time, and

she'd given him brief replies. Yes, she was fine, thanks. Yes, Constance's surgery had gone very well. And, yes, it was OK for her to keep Maple a while longer. Blunt. Brief. The way she was when she didn't want to deal with her emotions.

His fists clenched around the dog's lead as he walked into the building and a sweet old lady with a walking frame asked him something about Jetson. He replied on autopilot, distracted, wondering where Lucie was.

His eyes shot up to see her coming through the door behind him. Rising to attention, he raised a hand, hating how he forgave her lateness and everything else the second he saw her.

'Sorry, sorry... I was with Constance. She'll be out of the hospital soon, but we lost track of time discussing...'

She trailed off as he stood there, as if just seeing him had thrown her brain off track. He bit back a smile.

'You look good,' he told her, greeting Maple, straightening his shirt. He should have worn his other jeans, but Josiah had dropped yogurt on them before he'd even pulled them from the drying rack...

'You sound surprised,' she quipped. Her teeth caught her lower lip as she flicked her eyes to him. 'Maple's been helping me a lot.'

'No more nightmares, then?'

She hesitated. 'Like I said, she's been helping.'

Austin nodded, eyebrows raised at her. *Little victories*, he thought as they shared a moment that took him back to the sofa. Holding her. Hearing her cry.

There was nothing he could have done then to make her laugh. They weren't kids…he couldn't cartwheel now any better than he'd been able to back then. So he'd tried to fix it another way… asking her not to go back to all that. Almost kissing her.

She'd almost kissed him too. He'd had the distinct impression it was more than just her job and her need to leave the village that had stopped her, but he'd been trying not to dwell on it too much.

What did it matter now? She was going back, regardless of what he said.

'We're so excited you're here, Doctors,' a chatty nurse enthused, walking them through a sunlit corridor.

Paintings lined the walls: flowers, a windmill, a toad in welly boots. Mayflower was smaller and more exclusive than Lavender Springs. It had a kind of cosy wildlife theme going on that was a bit unusual. But Gramma May had a couple of friends in here, and his volunteers had brought dogs here before.

One lady with narcolepsy had used to keep one full time until she'd passed away—her cocker spaniel, Rigby, had proven to be the best way to detect an oncoming attack. Rigby had even learned to stand across her lap, to prevent her falling out of her wheelchair.

Austin admired Lucie's tight blue trousers and heeled boots, listening to her make amicable conversation with the nurse while her daffodil-yellow scarf wafted more perfume back his way. Everything about Lucie seemed designed to lure him in.

She really did seem to be looking better too, he noticed. Not as tired, and way more energetic. One step closer to getting back on the road? he thought, picturing Ruby's face. The twins were asking for her. Was it better to let them see her, or not? These were questions he was not equipped to answer.

'I take it you know all about Sundown Syndrome?' Lucie asked him, as they came to a stop by some floor-to-ceiling patio doors.

'Of course,' he said. 'Dementia can make people upset in the early evenings. It's a restless time. They get confused, and some of them wander about—'

'I know walking and talking helps,' she interjected. 'My patient here, Ethel, is a new arrival. She's a little lost at the best of times lately, but I thought we could try her with the dogs. She used to have one, I think.'

He knew what she was getting at. Maybe the dogs would distract this lady and help her to remember a few things.

'Talking helps,' he repeated, and he raised his eyebrows pointedly.

Talking with him at the house that night must have helped Lucie in some way. She probably didn't let those kinds of debilitating thoughts or feelings out to many people. At least she knew she could always talk to him—even if she'd never say what he wanted to hear.

The sea glimmered in the distance as he, Lucie and Ethel took to the gardens. Shrubs and flowers lined the concrete paths, and a bubbling water feature caught streaks of late sunshine in its ripples.

He walked with Ethel on his arm. She was beaming beneath a mop of wiry grey hair as if she'd won the lottery. Lucie walked at her other side.

'This is such a beautiful garden! You are so lucky you get to see all these flowers blooming, Ethel.'

Lucie seemed genuinely awed by the garden, and he caught himself smiling at her. She returned the smile at full wattage and the hint of tension lifted from between them.

They made light conversation on their walk around the rose bushes. Ethel kept stopping, looking around in confusion, her brow more wrinkled than it should have been. The dogs were playing and chasing each other, but Maple came back on command as Lucie stopped by the fountain. She'd noticed Ethel needed a distraction, as had he.

As they gathered around the fountain, Ethel's eyes soon moved to the dogs again. Sure enough, she started talking about the dog her husband had brought home once. 'It often came with us to a lovely pub in Staithes!'

'Did you go there a lot with your husband?' Lucie asked.

Austin followed with more questions, most of which Ethel answered quite articulately.

A nurse came to check all was well and raised her eyebrows on hearing Ethel talking, before leaving them to it.

Ethel told them all about her stint in the restaurant at the pub, when she'd waitressed there. She regaled them with the story of the day of a great storm that blew in and washed the seafront away.

'My husband was a fisherman. But that day he was plucking bottles of wine and beer from the water after the pub got flooded. The dog, too. Great at catching full beer bottles, he was.'

'Sounds like a smart dog. What was his name?' Lucie asked.

Ethel frowned. She got lost again for a moment.

'What colour was he?' Austin encouraged.

'Brown, of course.'

Lucie put a hand to her arm gently. 'What year was the storm, Ethel?'

'1953,' she said, without a beat.

Austin could barely suppress his grin. 'She's right,' he said, and Lucie laughed.

She blushed slightly as he touched a hand to her back before she stood up.

Another small, shared victory, and it felt like everything in that moment.

'Ethel's communicating more clearly than she has in days,' the nurse said later, hands on hips, impressed.

She bent to pat Maple, and Austin watched the pride flicker in Lucie's eyes, feeling it as if it were his own. It wasn't just Maple and Jetson who'd opened her up. Lucie's calming presence had been key. She was good at getting people to talk, even if she wasn't so good at it herself, he mused. Not about the truth behind her need to keep running, anyway. He knew there was more to it than their failed friendship, and more than her just not liking Brookborough. It shouldn't still get to him after all this time, but it did.

'We should walk the dogs before we go back,' Lucie suggested, as they made their way to the exit with a promise to stay longer next time. 'Unless you have to get back to the twins?'

'They're with Belle,' he replied.

It was impossible in that moment for him to concoct an excuse not to walk the dogs with her. And in minutes she was steering her car behind his on the narrow country road towards Staithes.

CHAPTER SEVENTEEN

PARKING WASN'T ALLOWED in the old town, due to the narrow streets. So Lucie parked her hire car by AJ's in the public car park near the station and they walked the winding lanes with the dogs towards the pub that Ethel had remembered—the Cod and Lobster.

They let the dogs run on the sand beneath the pub, and Lucie resisted bringing up that night at his house...the promise of a kiss that had shimmered between them but never eventuated. He probably regretted even thinking about it. *Ugh*, the humiliation.

She'd woken him up with her screaming, so he'd probably just been tired and confused. It was best not to say anything, she decided. Her own growing feelings were highly inconvenient, and she should do absolutely nothing to stir this pot any further.

Even being next to him again was excruciating. His snuggly knitted sweater was just the kind she'd have huddled into against the wind if she hadn't been trying her best to ignore their undeniable attraction and not make things harder for them both. Obviously until she'd called on him and the dogs to help Ethel out of her slump he'd been trying to keep his distance in light of her leaving, and she was going to respect that.

'Are you hungry?' he asked, breaking the silence.

Without either of them saying it, Lucie knew they would be heading back to the Cod and Lobster.

They ordered battered cod and mushy peas and chips. While the dogs salivated, Lucie wondered if there would ever be a time when she would look at AJ and *not* find him the sexiest guy on earth. So different from the boy she'd once known.

'Remember your crab races?' she said, recalling the buckets of the snappy creatures he'd used to collect from the rock pools.

'Remember the first time we found fool's gold?'

He grinned, and she sat back in her seat as a flood of the best kind of memories washed over her. A sense of belonging was slowly creeping in. She wrestled with it, but it kept on winning. It felt kind of nice. More than nice.

'I tried to convince everyone at school that my gold was real,' AJ said, smiling.

They'd both been fascinated by those shiny little nuggets of iron pyrite that looked so much like the real thing.

'If only it *had* been real...' She sighed.

'What would you do with all the gold in the world?' he asked her.

His warm blue eyes twinkled in the firelight from the open hearth. It was dark outside now.

'Buy your house,' she replied without a beat. 'And give it to you.'

He bit his cheek. 'It's paid off,' he admitted, omitting the information that Ebby's life insurance had covered most of it. 'I told you—it's just too big. We need something smaller now Belle's moving in with Bryce.'

'I'm sure you could fill it,' she said, serious now.

It had been playing on her mind for days—the house he loved going up for sale. It didn't feel right. Probably because she loved it, too, and also because she knew the twins would be moving from the only place they remembered living in.

A feeling of displacement threatened her calm. She should know how to be a rock for a family who'd lost so much. She'd pretty much walked her childhood in their shoes.

'Aren't there a few more dogs you could adopt?' she asked.

Maybe she could help them find a solution.

He shrugged. 'Let me guess… That sounds like your worst nightmare? A house full of kids and dogs…'

Lucie bristled, glancing at the sleeping dogs. 'I've had worse nightmares—as you well know.'

'But fewer, lately?' he probed. 'Since you talked to me?'

'Since I got Maple.' She winced. 'OK...*and* since I talked to you.'

She bit her lip. How did he know?

She hadn't exactly admitted it before now, but he was right. She shrugged. So what if she'd slept better since talking to him? It didn't mean she'd be relying on him for anything else. The only person she could count on was herself, she reminded herself. Though somehow it didn't quite ring as true as it had used to.

'As for having a house full of kids and dogs,' she continued, 'I don't think I've ever really let myself think beyond the next place I might unpack a suitcase.'

'Why not? Why do you always have to keep going? All on your own?'

'I'm not on my own. I have my team.'

'You know what I mean, Lucie.'

She paused, open-mouthed, ready to make a biting remark in self-defence. Then she realised she didn't really have one.

AJ eyed her thoughtfully. 'It's OK to want to stay in one place, you know,' he said. 'You don't have to keep putting your own life in danger just because you couldn't save your teammate—which wasn't your fault, by the way.'

'Who died and made you my therapist?' she snapped, taking a gulp of water.

AJ sat back in his seat. 'Sorry,' he said to the bobbing boats outside the windows.

He wasn't sorry though. And she knew he had the right to give her his brutal honesty. Their history had given him that right long ago and there was nothing she could do about it.

'I just don't think you should go back to something just because you feel guilty, Lucie.'

'Is that the only reason you don't want me to go back?' she shot back, surprised at her own courage. *Silence.*

She continued, 'I wouldn't make a good mother figure, AJ. You know that.'

AJ let out a loud snort of indignation. 'Is that what you think? That I'm trying to replace Ebby with *you*?'

Blood rushed to her cheeks but she kept a straight face. 'I don't know.' She turned her eyes to the view through the big glass windows. 'You almost kissed me that night in your living room, after my dream.'

Her heart was like a hopping rabbit. Of course it would slip out. And now he knew she'd been thinking about it.

AJ cleared his throat. 'I did.'

She swallowed—hard. What exactly was she fishing for here? She'd decided not to go there, and he already regretted it, judging by the look on his face.

'I just don't want you going back out to disaster

zones,' he said measuredly. 'That's no secret. I've seen what it's done to you. But I'm not looking to trap you into marriage, if that's what you think. Maybe you've just opened my eyes to some... stuff.'

'Oh, yes?'

Oh, God.

'I can't keep living in the past. I don't want to any more.' He rearranged his napkin on the table, lifted one eyebrow in an imperious arch. 'I kind of feel...guilty about this, you know? But maybe I *am* finally ready to date someone.'

Her heart lurched, but she kept her face in check. 'Someone who'd be good for the kids?' she managed. Nausea ate at her from the inside as the thought of it took her mind hostage. 'Good for you.'

'Of course Ruby and Josiah will come into all my decisions,' he said carefully.

She frowned. 'You should do what's right for *you*, AJ.'

'Ditto.'

'And you don't have to feel guilty about that.'

'Neither should you feel guilty for living your life when your friend lost his.'

'Mmm...'

Lucie played with her phone, pretending to answer an important email. She feigned indifference to the thought of him dating, while her jealous heart roared. Who would he date now that she'd riled him up and made him see he was ready to let someone in? Who would win his heart when she'd disappeared again?

Definitely better not to think about that. Especially if Claire Bainbridge is still single.

'So, it looks like you're enjoying Maple being around,' he said next, signalling for the bill.

Lucie swallowed, and admitted that, yes, the dog was helping her exponentially, actually.

Although the truth was letting it all out onto AJ's shoulders back at the house the other week was what had really put her on the path to healing. He was right about that. It felt so good to have got it all out, to have someone who knew her really *hear* her.

'Hopefully you can find her a new foster home before I leave,' she found herself saying, as he paid the bill.

If only her stomach would stop tying itself into knots.

AJ grunted something indecipherable, pulling on his jacket.

Cringing, she cursed herself. She'd stupidly said that on purpose, to distance herself more. Because the worst had already happened in her head. His marriage to the new amazing woman who'd make all his thoughts about *her* disappear into the ether. There was someone out there just waiting to fire up his bloodstream. He was pulling away from her faster than she could push him.

They were halfway back to the cars with the dogs, in an orange-lit cobbled alleyway, when she realised her tears were causing serious vision impairment. She blinked them away, but it was too late. AJ had seen.

Blinking again, she watched his face come into view, close up, concerned…almost angry. It was suddenly all too much. She had to tell him why she'd left all those years ago.

'AJ…' She felt words piling up on top of themselves in her throat. There was nowhere for them to go any more, other than out. 'You humiliated me, AJ! I trusted you!'

AJ balked. 'What do you mean? What are you talking about? When did I do that?'

'With Claire Bainbridge! I heard you that night, in your room. I came to talk to you about Aunt Lina's offer to pay for my tuition if I went back to Denver…and I heard you and Claire, talking and laughing about me.'

AJ took a step back, but Lucie closed the space between them.

'She said I followed you around like a little lost puppy…that I was cramping your style. And you said nothing to defend me! I thought we were friends, and you let her speak about me like that. You were more interested in sleeping with her—'

'Wait!' He ran his hands across his head and jaw, glowering. 'You overheard that?'

'I didn't mean to! I left before I had to hear you guys having sex.'

'We didn't have sex!' He stared at her now, incredulous. 'So *that's* why you decided never to speak to me again once you went to America? Lucie, I didn't need to defend you to her, or to anyone, because what we had was nobody else's business. If you'd stuck around for long enough, you would have heard me tell her that. I certainly did *not* sleep with her!'

Lucie gaped at him, feeling heat and mortification creep through every bone in her body, turning her legs to jelly. She sank against a brick wall.

He followed her, forcing her into his shadow, towering over her. 'You left Brookborough, and me, because of *that*? Lucie…'

'You were *everything* to me!'

'*You* were everything to *me*.'

She lunged for him with an aching desperation, and their hands and bodies suddenly intertwined in a tangled embrace. He took her hair in his fists and kissed her fiercely, with all of his soul, till she felt as if she was underwater, pulled along by the tide of him, swept away.

'Lucie…' he moaned against her mouth.

She dissolved into a thousand tiny shards of longing as he moaned her name.

AJ pinned her against a shuttered storefront and the streetlight shone in her face, creating a silhouette of him. Her back rasped against the rough wooden door, jingling a tiny bell that she ignored. His hands slid across her body with intent now, stirring a fire in her chest, igniting her flesh under her clothes. He was her everything… he'd been her everything…and she wanted him so badly it hurt.

Their breaths were coming hot and hungry, like a fire finding its way back up from burnt-out embers. When AJ stopped for just a moment, as if to absorb her, she saw his eyes were transformed in the streetlight. A craving she'd never seen before shone back at her.

Arching further into him, she felt her body vibrate with need. Her hips sought his, pressing against him as if she might slip into his skin, and a flood of hot moisture filled her core. If they hadn't been out on the street she might have laid him down and demanded he show her what he'd never shown her before—she would have gladly taken it…she'd waited for ever for this.

It was only when a passing stranger cleared his throat that they sprang apart. Her mouth was full of the taste of him. It wasn't enough. Ramming her hands through her hair, she caught her breath as AJ adjusted his sweater, then his jeans.

'I didn't mean for that to happen,' she managed, when the stranger had gone.

Her words were futile. Actions spoke far louder. Neither of them could have stopped if they'd tried. Even the dogs looked as if they were judging them.

'We shouldn't have done that…' She tried again, coming to her senses, but he was stepping towards her, determined.

'Neither of us is dating anyone else, are we?'

'Not yet.' She sighed out her frustration, her lips still stinging. 'But I'm no good for you.'

He cupped her face in one hand, drawing her to him firmly. A shuddering exhalation left her throat.

'Why don't you let me decide what's good for me while you're still here?'

'You don't mean that, AJ. This will only get complicated.'

'Maybe it will.'

His determination cancelled out her next string of excuses. He was willing to take the risk if she was. It was written all over his face.

He brought his mouth to hers and she lost herself in him all over again. They could kiss, she supposed. It didn't have to mean anything. Besides, they were good at it. *Very* good at it. His tongue aroused primordial parts of her that felt as if they'd been in hibernation for years. Oh, the places his tongue could go…

They *wouldn't* do anything else, though, she warned herself. No going home with him, or her resolve would be ruined. She had to be strong and let kisses be enough.

CHAPTER EIGHTEEN

THE PROBLEM WITH kissing Lucie, Austin thought, opening the car door for her, was that it wasn't enough. Now he wanted more.

Constance could see it on their faces the second she answered the door—he was sure of it. The two women made small talk like old friends while he made tea and Lucie performed her check-ups. And although Constance was weary, with a lingering loss of appetite after her straightforward surgery to remove the tumour, she fed treats to Maple—her favourite—and asked Lucie about Gramma May.

'So how are things with you?' Constance asked him as they all took their seats in the living room.

The little green sofa felt even smaller than last time, when he'd sat down on it with Lucie. A flyer for the Paws Under the Stars event sat on the coffee table—not long to go now. Maple was going to be Yoda. As for Jetson…he was still waiting for Josiah and Ruby to decide.

'I should be asking you that,' he told Constance, ignoring the little wink she shot him.

Was it obvious to her that something had happened between him and Lucie?

Just a little taste of Lucie before he got back on the dating scene—that was what he'd been telling himself their kiss had been. But all he'd been able to think about since that kiss was Lucie—which was exactly why he *had* to find someone else. Surely it would be better to have someone lined up to distract him when the crushing absence of her kicked in again?

They hadn't told a soul about that kiss, but everyone seemed to know something was up. Gramma May was giving him looks whenever she saw him and the twins. And Gramma May had told Cynthia something, and Cynthia had told everyone who wandered into the chocolate shop. Even if they only cared about chocolates.

He'd agonised over it—the fact that Lucie had left Brookborough thinking his loyalties lay with Claire Bainbridge instead of her. But even though he'd as good as said she was his world back then, she'd backed off, still convinced she should be somewhere else. Well, he wasn't about to beg her to stay if she didn't want to. She wasn't good for him—she was damn right about that. Not when she was a fleeting ship just passing by this village.

But instead of doing what he should be doing—which was keeping far away, where he couldn't get burnt—he'd arranged to work with her again. They were a good team, after all—the patients loved her, and that *was* why they were here. Clearly he was also a glutton for punishment.

'I just had to see you and Jetson,' Constance told him now, over her teacup. 'You know, you both might have saved my life. How can I ever thank you?'

'Your good health is thanks enough…it's what we're here for,' Austin told her, feeling himself tense as Lucie's eyes rested on his profile.

'All I can think about is how grateful I am for Thera Pups, Dr Johnstone, and I'd like to donate, or help in any way I can. Sponsor a dog, maybe…?'

Lucie reached for her hand as the woman's voice faltered. 'You don't have to do that.'

'I just… I'm going to miss you.'

'We can come and see you for as long as you need.'

'There are plenty of people who need you more—and the dogs.' Constance's hand found Jetson's furry ears, and the dog promptly put his big soft head in her lap.

'Just because other people need us too, it doesn't mean we won't still find time for you,' Lucie assured her.

Until you leave us all, Austin thought begrudgingly, wishing he didn't keep on getting hit so hard by the thought of it. She wouldn't find time for *anyone* here when she was gone again. The sooner he got used to that, the better.

'How much longer do we have you for, Lucie?'

Constance seemed sad at the prospect of losing her, too.

'A few weeks,' she admitted, glancing his way.

The two of them had clearly talked about her 'real' job. A chill coursed up his spine, and he fought the sudden nausea that roiled in his stomach.

'And where do you go on your next mission? I think it's so wonderful what you do. Don't you, Dr Johnstone?'

He nodded mutely, focusing on the dogs, ignoring Lucie's eyes drilling into him. Constance seemed excited for her. But all he could do was stop the resentment from showing on his face as she answered, 'I don't know where I'll be placed just yet.'

She could build her world right here. People would love her and need her just as much as they would in some as yet undetermined but no doubt dangerous location across the globe. But she didn't want to do that.

Lucie's phone buzzed through her jacket. As she pulled it out, her face showed confusion. 'Lavender Springs…' she frowned. 'Belle says Jack Granger has asked for me and Maple.'

Oh, really?

Austin watched as she tapped into the phone. Their elderly stroke patient was obviously having a bad day and he'd directly asked for Lucie. She'd made even more of an impression on people than he had thought. Pride swelled through him—before the dread set in. It wasn't just himself and the twins and Gramma May who'd miss her.

'I should go,' she said.

'And go you must,' Constance said with a good-natured sigh, ruffling Maple's ears.

Austin called to Jetson. Jack had been *his* patient first, and he would be again when Lucie disappeared.

'I'll go with you,' he declared, leaving her absolutely no room to argue.

Belle met them in Reception. 'Thank God you're here!'

She ushered them and the dogs through to a private room, where Jack Granger sat in an armchair, staring with melancholy out of the window.

'He says his heart hurts,' she whispered. 'We haven't seen any immediate signs of cardiovascular issues, but…'

'We'll check him out,' AJ said.

The dogs had already padded over to Jack, who was so far ignoring them.

'Hey, Jack,' Lucie said in concern, crouching beside his chair. 'Your heart hurts? Will you let us take you through to another room, so we can check you out?'

'You won't find anything,' he replied, finally acknowledging them.

'You don't know that,' AJ said.

'Yes, I do. It's just Alice. She has a habit of doing this thing to my heart. She died on this day, you know. I feel her on the day…every year.'

Lucie put a hand to AJ's arm. Both dogs lay at Jack's feet, as if they were perfectly happy to bide their time.

'Silly, I know,' Jack continued. 'But I'd rather be with a dog right now than *any* human.' He glanced at Lucie. 'They listen. They know our hearts. At least, mine always used to.'

Austin caught Lucie's look.

'Something about having a dog keeps me calm, too,' she replied. 'Which, in turn, makes me think about things more rationally.'

Jack nodded.

Lucie went on. 'I think I told you on my last visit that the dogs have helped me so much, since I got back to the village. And they'll always be here to listen to you, too.'

Austin's heartbeat skidded. Was she trying to hammer home the fact that she was almost ready to leave them?

'She would have liked you, my Alice,' Jack said, as his leathery hand reached for Jetson's ear.

His bad arm was still in a sling, but the man had more colour in his cheeks than the last time Austin had seen him, and he seemed to be talking more to Lucie than he ever had to him.

'How long were you married?' he cut in, determined to strike up a rapport.

Jack sighed. 'Over fifty years. I never remarried. Never did find anybody quite like her. She was a dancer...'

They listened as Jack spoke about courting Alice, calmed and encouraged by the dogs' gentle presence. Before half an hour had passed they had him out on a short walk and throwing a ball for the dogs in the garden by the shallow duck pond.

Lucie took Austin aside. 'Are you OK? Hearing this stuff?' she whispered in concern.

'Stuff?' He feigned ignorance.

It should be a good thing that he didn't feel quite as jarred by the subject of losing a spouse as he would have done a few months or even weeks ago. Lucie had a lot to do with that, he supposed. For all the good it would do him when she was gone again.

'I'm OK,' he assured her stiltedly.

'You're allowed to talk about Ebby if you want,' she replied, clearly reading him all wrong. 'It's healthy. Talking about Alice has just helped Jack.'

'I'm not Jack,' he said, frustration making him snap. 'Maybe I just don't want to talk about it, Lucie. Not with you.'

Lucie looked hurt and he squared his shoulders, turning away towards Jack. He felt bad immediately. He shouldn't have snapped at her. But she had no idea that the way he'd felt for his late wife had never matched the extent and depth of his long-hidden love for Lucie. And even now there was nothing he could do to change that.

Belle caught his arm on the way out. 'Austin, are we still on for tonight? I have some great ideas for your new dating profile!'

His stomach plummeted.

Lucie's eyes grew wide. Then she turned and feigned uninterest as Belle winked at him.

'When the twins are in bed we'll go over it,' she said. 'I'm working on making you sound like the most eligible bachelor in town. Not that he isn't—right, Lucie?'

'Sorry…what?' Lucie was stroking Maple, pretending not to listen.

He felt his lips twitch at the look on her face. Sure, Belle was stirring the pot—trying to suss out what was going on with them following the rumours—but poor Lucie was clearly seething inside now, her cheeks red as cherry sorbet under her make-up.

'We're getting this boy back on the market!' Belle grinned, ruffling his hair.

'I'm not some prize bull, Belle,' he told her gruffly, shaking her off, daring another look at Lucie.

Her lips were a thin, jealous line. She was bashing at her phone with furious, stabbing motions, as if she wished it was his face.

It hadn't exactly been his intention to make her

jealous. In fact, up until this moment his own pent-up frustration had left a bitter taste in his mouth. He should just get her out of his head *and* his life for good and move on. Why live in the past when he had to focus on the future? Especially when that future wasn't going to involve Ebby *or* Lucie.

But the look on her face! It *was* mildly entertaining, seeing how much she actually cared. Maybe she didn't want to get out of here as much as she liked to think she did?

'You couldn't even wait till I'm gone?' she said coolly, as soon as they were outside.

The spring sunshine infused the air with warmth, and the sky was a vivid blue now the rain seemed to be behind them. The dogs sped on ahead into the garden, towards the pond again, and he followed them—they clearly needed a longer run before getting back in the car.

'Are you jealous?' he dared, unable to stop the grin from spreading across his face.

'I'm not jealous,' she hissed. A couple of geese flapped in a panic, moving away from the oncoming dogs. 'But I know you're just doing this to antagonise me, Austin.'

'You know, you only call me Austin when you're angry,' he teased.

Her hands flew up in the air as she walked across the grass beside him. 'Whatever. I don't care what you do.'

'Yes, you do. And anyway, this is all Belle. I don't know why you're angry with me. She just wants to help me out.'

'So let her. I'm sure she'll line you up with a whole string of dates before the week is out. You can have your pick.'

'Maybe so,' he said, stopping in his tracks by the pond. 'But none of them will be you.'

Lucie sniffed, looked at him askance, then rolled her eyes.

'You're cute when you're jealous,' he said.

A flicker of a smile took over her face, but then she scowled, staring at the ducks. 'I'm not cute.'

'Aha! You just admitted you're jealous.' He prodded her side and she squealed and jumped back, laughing.

'You're such an idiot!'

She pushed him playfully with both hands. His foot slid on the wet grass.

Oh, no!

Before he knew what was happening, he was splashing into the pond, ducks and geese flapping everywhere. The dogs barked furiously, thinking it was a game.

'Oh, my God, AJ!' Lucie's hands flew to her mouth as she ran to the edge. 'I'm so sorry! Here, take my—'

He waded over, took her outstretched hand. But instead of using it to pull himself out he pulled her into the water with him. Lucie screamed and flailed her arms, landing backwards, and he couldn't help it. He cracked up. He could barely stand up in the waist-high water, he was laughing so hard.

'What are you…? AJ, I can't *believe* you!' she gasped, scraping back her wet hair, blinking as mascara streaked her face.

She splashed him, and he reciprocated, until they were sloshing water wildly at each other, laughing hysterically. Deep belly laughs ricocheted through him at the utter ridiculousness of the situation—he hadn't laughed this hard in *years*.

'Was that payback for that day you arrived?' he asked through his tears of laughter.

She waded towards him. Her shirt was totally see-through.

Hot. Damn.

'It was an accident and you know it. *This*, on the other hand, pulling me into the pond, was not an accident. Look at me!'

'It was funny, though,' he said, as his laughter subsided. He found her waist and pulled her close possessively, tracing the outline of her bra through her shirt with his eyes. 'And I am looking at you. Why do you have to be so sexy?' he growled.

Lucie caught her breath. He waited for her to push him away, but she moaned softly, pressed her hips to his under the warm water…an invitation. For a moment they stood there, breathing deeply, forehead to forehead. Excruciating.

*Do not kiss her. Do not go there. You'll be a
total idiot if you do this again...*

It was hard to tell who kissed who first. Lucie
gripped the front of his sodden shirt, tugging him
closer, opening her mouth to him. The feel of her
set a wildfire alight in his veins that should have
evaporated every drop of water in the pond.

Then self-deprecation came crashing in too, as
they kissed. He shouldn't want her...should not
still be doing this. She'd said it herself. She was
no good for him...

Except in this moment she was everything.

Their mouths crashed, exploring, tongues twirling, sucking, licking, groaning. Half a decade he'd
waited, to feel an ounce of what he was feeling
around her. Half a decade. Wasn't that long enough
to have let the darkness and rage and helplessness
consume all his fire? Wasn't it the point of life? To
love, and be loved, even if that love was fleeting?

Lucie pulled back first, breaking their kiss to
run her eyes over his face. They told him she was
hungry for more of him, but her hands had stopped
roving up and down his back and were now resting
firmly around his shoulders. She put her forehead
back against his. His fingers traced the contours
of her beautiful face. She exhaled deeply, as if all
the world's problems were escaping her.

'I want you.'

'I guess we should get out of this pond then,'
he responded.

Another giggle escaped her mouth.

'I'd actually forgotten we were in the pond,' he admitted, pulling out his shirt, only to find it slapping back, cold and wet against his skin.

She stuck out her tongue as he swept her fringe aside. The deep affection and longing in her eyes struck him to the core before she looked away, hugging herself.

He could still read her after all these years. Leaving him was going to be hard for her—harder than she was letting on. Even harder now. But if this was really all he could have of her, he suddenly wanted all he could get while he could.

'You can expect an invoice for another pair of boots ruined!' she huffed playfully, wading back to the bank, with him following close behind.

It wasn't till they were standing on the edge, wringing out their clothes and their hair, that he realised several people, including Belle, were standing at the large window of the care home, laughing and clapping in delight.

'And they thought the dogs coming was the most exciting thing to have happened all week,' Lucie said, wiping the mascara from her cheeks and daring a wave.

Grinning, he waved too. 'I think we gave them something to talk about,' he said, trying not to think about the questions Belle would no doubt have for him later.

Luckily she'd be at work for another few hours,

and the twins were going on an after-school play-date at a friend's house.

He took Lucie's hand. Her fingers curled around his. They locked eyes.

'There's no one at my place,' he said, cocking an eyebrow.

Lucie closed her eyes and nodded.

Together, still laughing, they hurried back to the car, the dogs sprinting after them. Slamming the door shut, Lucie leaned across the gearstick and pressed her mouth to his.

'Are you sure you want to come back with me?' he asked her, mid-kiss.

Her wandering hands between his legs was the only answer he needed.

CHAPTER NINETEEN

AJ's BREATHING WAS the only sound in the room. It mingled with her own hot gasps at the feel of him, his muscles, his hard lines and sounds and touches. The way he kissed her, with her back pressed to the cool bird's-egg-blue of the bedroom wall. It drove her mad for him.

Downstairs, music sang from the stereo and for a second Lucie feared the twins might come darting up the stairs, demanding something. But they weren't home.

It was just them, and there was no going back now—not after that kiss in the pond. And not after the steamy shower they'd just shared...all the foreplay. He'd tasted parts of her no one had tasted in a while, and he was definitely not the awkward teen she'd first fallen for. Every atom of her being wanted—no, *needed* him—all of the amazing adult AJ. Just once. Just this one time.

He was urging her to the bed, his hands roaming with intent across her sides and back, kissing, stroking, caressing her, and then teasing away the towel he'd given her just seconds before in the bathroom.

'Do you even know how crazy you make me?' he uttered in equal awe and frustration.

Desire was written all over his face as he took her in, naked and sprawled beneath him across the sheets. It didn't cross her mind to feel self-conscious, but an overwhelming flood of emotion threatened to steal the moment as she looked into his eyes.

No. She would not admit how much his honesty moved her—how much this sense of connection and of comfort made her question every solo plan and goal she'd ever made for herself. That would be getting in far too deep.

She didn't know where she was going next. That had never been an issue before…going into the unknown. It was the thought of staying here that got to her, she realised solemnly, as this new-found intimacy threatened to make her cry. God, his mouth, his eyes…she could fall into him and keep falling…

'You're amazing…you know that?' she said, meaning it, stroking his bottom lip with her thumb, memorising every detail of his face.

She was falling already. But what if she let herself go, offered it all up, and then he decided *no.* She'd be broken. She'd have to leave anyway— she owed it to Jorge—but she'd leave with her heart doubly broken. Like after Mum and Dad had died…when she was sent to England.

'I wish I could get inside your brain,' he said, kissing her eyes softly.

He traced the lines of her mouth with his thumb, sending a current through her bloodstream. Suddenly her whole body zinged and burned for him, hot, sticky and ready. This was not a time for emotions.

Get a grip. Just enjoy it.

She dared to nibble on one forefinger, sucking it into her mouth, twirling her tongue around it—a teaser. She smiled at him, taking all of him in, savouring the sound of his deep, throaty moan as he stroked her hair.

AJ didn't want to wait a moment longer and neither did she. But it wasn't good to rush these things, she thought. Not if they were only going to do this once.

Hovering over her, AJ murmured her name against the smooth skin of her ear, brushed her damp hair away to reveal more flesh, whispering how much he wanted her against her lips, and kissing his way down to her inner thighs.

She shuddered as his mouth explored below her hips, and when he leaned across her to fumble in a drawer for protection she kissed her way along his arms, up to the contours of his torso. The familiarity and the mystery of him combined was such a turn-on she couldn't stand it.

Rolling her over to her side, he spooned her, his hardness pressed to her back, and for a moment they slowed.

'Something tells me you like it like this,' he murmured, sending a spark and a thrill of anticipation bolting through her, so delicious it was almost unbearable.

'I do,' she encouraged, arching back into him.

Lucie bit down on her hand to stop her cries of pleasure giving them away to the neighbours as he entered her, rocking slowly at first. She felt herself swelling around him, her body accepting his, welcoming him, expanding and contracting to please him. God…how had she ever left without telling him how much she wanted this? How had she given up without even trying?

They might have made love for thirty minutes or an hour—who could remember? Sometimes their eyes were closed, when they were lost in the moment and each divine sensation. Sometimes they locked eyes, tried new positions, then laughed and tried more. He seemed intent on pleasuring her, making sure he was the best she'd ever had, and all she wanted to do was make him remember her. For ever.

He would think about her when she was gone… when he was filling in that dating profile. Or maybe he wouldn't… This was one afternoon of fun—not love…not something to carry into for ever.

He's never told you he loves you.

She shoved the thought away to deal with it later, letting him worship her. She kissed him for every single moment he'd missed her, when she'd left him to go to America. Kept him close inside her for all the times he'd felt broken and alone. Pressed her hands to his heart and kept to his rhythm, knowing she'd be conjuring up this memory for months and years to come. Wherever she ended up next, she would take this moment with her.

AJ threw himself into her. They were both in the fire now. But it wasn't as if they could help it. He'd decided, as she had, to accept that they were just going to burn…

'Where were you? There's a letter on the sideboard for you,' Gramma May said later, when she finally made her way home.

AJ had made it pretty clear that she needed to be gone before the twins were dropped home after their play date. But walking away from the house had been tough.

And now she was starting to think she might have made a big, fat, stupid mistake, telling herself she could leave permanently again with zero consequences. Her head was still reeling…the taste and smell of him was all over her like a coat she didn't want to take off.

She swiped up the envelope. The handwriting wasn't familiar. Opening it, she felt only half present. She was changed, somehow—different from the woman who'd left for work that morning. While he hadn't exactly said he loved her... he'd never say that...she could have sworn she saw it in his eyes.

Gramma May met her in the kitchen as she poured a glass of water. Her throat was parched.

'You were with Austin all day?'

'I was,' she replied, filling up Maple's water bowl and running her hands through her fur as she lapped at the liquid with her tongue.

Crouched beside Maple, Lucie finally read the letter. Her hand stopped dead in the dog's fur as a small bookmark fluttered out. Her own face beamed up at her, alongside Jorge's. The picture had been taken just weeks before he'd lost his life. The letter was from Jorge's widow, asking when she'd be back in Peru. She had a gift for her: a memorial book she'd had made for all the victims of the earthquake, too heavy to mail.

It was months ago that Lucie had given permission for some of the photos from their operation to be included in it.

Thank you, Lucie, for your continued work for MRO. I bet you can't wait to get back out there!

Jorge would be so proud of you—as am I.

I hope you're enjoying your well-deserved break in England.

Love, Maria

Her hands were shaking.

Gramma May was still talking. 'Cynthia texted me. Her mother was at Lavender Springs, visiting a friend today. She said some couple put on quite a show in the pond, after they fell in. Would you know anything about that?'

'What?'

Lucie barely heard her…her nerves were shot. Just when she'd allowed herself to feel good, maybe even to contemplate staying here longer, to see how things went with AJ, here was yet another reminder that she had a life and responsibilities elsewhere.

Thanks a lot, universe!

'You know what I'm talking about.' Gramma May rolled her eyes, then frowned. 'So, you're back together, are you?'

She pulled hot sheets out of the tumble dryer and loaded them into a basket. Lucie shoved the letter into a kitchen drawer and sprang to her feet to take over the chore.

'We never got together in the first place, Gramma,' she informed her, realising her cheeks were probably flaming red, and her hair was a dishevelled mess.

'You didn't? I thought you must have. I don't know… He always carried a torch for you.'

She was taken aback. 'Did he?'

Gramma May rolled her eyes. 'The two of you belong together. Cynthia said it was the highlight of their day at Lavender, the pair of you in the pond. I quote, "Like something from a great romance." The residents can't wait to see their favourite couple again. With the dogs, of course. They've never had such a laugh.'

Lucie swallowed a pang. 'We're not a couple,' she reminded her.

'Tell that to the ducks in the pond. Sounds like they got a close-up look at your antics.'

'It was just a kiss…' Lucie trailed off, folding a sheet all wrong, then starting again.

It had *started* with a kiss, anyway.

'Don't mess with his heart,' Gramma May said suddenly, and Lucie flinched. 'That poor boy has been through enough.'

The severity of her tone shook her.

Lucie sank to a chair, dropping her head into her hands as the flood of oxytocin and adrenaline from the amazing sex with AJ evaporated with a *poof.*

Of course Gramma was right.

'I don't mean to say *you* haven't been through a lot, too,' Gramma May added kindly, stopping her folding to place a hand to her arm. 'But he's the one who has to stay here and lose you all over again when you go.'

'He's a big boy, Gramma, he knows what he's doing,' she retorted, thinking of the online dating profile Belle would assist him with creating.

The thought of it stole her last remnants of happiness after the love they'd just made, along with her breath. Gramma May looked worried now, and Lucie flinched again.

Moments like this, when she felt like such a burden, reminded her of how sad Gramma had sounded, telling Cynthia she'd never travelled with Grampa Bert and now she never would—all because of her.

'You don't have to go,' Gramma said, as if sensing her melancholy. 'You know that, don't you, pet? If you have something good here…'

Lucie blinked, struggling to form a thought in her head. Gramma was sweet…always so sweet. And AJ was a very good thing that she had here. But… She didn't have him, exactly. He hadn't so much as hinted that this afternoon wasn't just a one-off, a chance to see what they'd missed out on all those years ago. He was looking for a woman who had experience with young children…

'Did you hear me?'

'Yes…yes, Gramma. And, yes, I know I don't *have* to go back. But it's my job.'

'Get another job.'

'It's not that easy.'

'Yes, it is. You could work with AJ. He's doing some wonderful things.'

'I have to go.'

'Go where, exactly?'

'I don't know yet!'

Gramma May made a *pfft* sound, and mumbled, 'Doesn't sound like a great job to me.'

Lucie's arms trembled in her still-damp shirt-sleeves as she made her way upstairs.

That night, when AJ called her, she texted back, saying that she was tired. She wrote Thanks for a fun afternoon and cursed at the moon through the window.

Gramma May was worried for AJ's heart. But *she* was going to be hurt more. AJ would be fine... he was the most eligible bachelor in town! Any woman would be mad not to snap him up, pin him down...just like she'd pinned him down in bed earlier.

Oh, God, that had been so amazing! Better than she'd dreamed it would be—better than they would've been as awkward teenagers together, surely.

But this was just a bubble she was passing through dreamily on a foamy wave, like the remnants of the great storm that Ethel had talked about.

Jorge's face when the walls came down... She would never un-see that. Not until she'd got back out there—back where it had happened, maybe? People were expecting her back, relying on her! She was needed.

Her message had to be clear.

It was really special, AJ, but it can't happen again and you know it.

He replied after some time.

I hate it when you're right.

Turning her phone over, she left it at that.
That night, the nightmares rushed back with a vengeance.

CHAPTER TWENTY

AUSTIN TURNED HIS face to the sky, listening to the soft banter between Ruby and Josiah. They were negotiating turns on the bouncy helicopter ride. The play park in Dalby Forest was busy this Sunday, now it was coming into late April, and this morning's organised dog walk had twenty-three attendees so far. Here was another one now.

The car door swung open and Lucie stepped out into the sunshine with Maple. A silent groan formed in his throat. Trust her to look amazing for a forest walk. Sheer tights showed off her legs under a short skirt. A light denim jacket swung from one hand. She'd been invited by Samuel's mother, who wanted to talk with them both about Bingo, now their live-in beagle.

'Lucie!' The twins rushed to greet her and started patting an enthusiastic Maple through the fence.

Austin fanned himself with his sweater, waiting for the usual cloud of tension to descend from the clear blue sky.

'Hey, guys!' Lucie looked good in pink lipstick as she high-fived the twins over the low play park fence. 'Are you excited for this dog walk your dad's organised? I didn't know you were coming.'

She shot him a telling sideways glance and he shrugged. 'Belle was busy.'

They gabbled on at her and he watched with interest as they interacted. Ruby especially was excited to see Lucie. She couldn't wait to tell her absolutely everything she'd been doing over the last couple of weeks all in one enthusiastic breath.

It wasn't a great feeling. He'd been extra-careful since they'd slept together at the house not to let the twins get close to her. He and Lucie had continued working together, of course. They were adults. They could cope without acting on their attraction. But only just...

It wasn't exactly easy—at least not for him—knowing they'd done that...in his bed...to each other's bodies...after so many years of wondering. And now she was all set to leave again. He knew he probably wouldn't have gone that far with anyone else *but* Lucie—which didn't help his guilt.

The walkers showed up one by one. Some were his volunteers, but not all of them had dogs. Some had kids and relatives who needed a little animal therapy in the fresh air.

'It's so great that Thera Pups does this for everyone,' Lucie said when they'd set off as a group down the wide forest track.

The sunlight dappled her hair through the canopy. Songbirds tweeted their approval of the warm weather.

'Every other weekend…late April through to September,' he told her, noting how Josiah had struck up a conversation with Samuel, up ahead, and was now throwing sticks for Bingo. Samuel's mother was chatting with Tom, who ran the model railway shop.

'They take after you,' Lucie said, looking with affection at Josiah. 'They'll be working for Thera Pups before you know it.'

'Maybe…who knows?' he said. 'I added Jetson's cancer detection in Constance to my latest paper. It's got a lot of people pretty excited.'

She raised her eyebrows in interest. Encouraged, he told her about a few potential investors for a training programme similar to his in the States. In turn, she told him how Ethel had asked for him and Jetson today at the Mayflower Care Home. And then she told him how Cynthia had probed her earlier, in the chocolate shop, about the pond incident at Lavender Springs.

He cleared his throat, not sure what to say. All he'd wanted to do every night since that day was show up and bang on her door. Now, the second she locked eyes with him and blew her fringe away, it was obvious that even in their recent forced indifference it had been playing heavily on her mind too.

'Are you OK?' she asked, lowering her voice to a whisper barely audible over the rustling trees.

'We're pretty good at being professional,' he replied carefully. Then he glanced at her sideways. 'Except around duck ponds.'

'That's not what I meant but...those poor ducks,' she added softly.

He smirked as they crossed the wooden slats of a bridge. His pillows had carried her scent for days afterwards, and he was ashamed to admit he hadn't washed the sheets until he'd absolutely *had* to.

'The twins keep asking about you.'

'I've kind of missed their energy,' she admitted.

Oh, really?

He watched her face for signs that she was just saying that because she thought she should. She seemed genuine, though. His heart began to thud wildly as he held his hand out to help her jump down from the bridge.

He looked around them. No one was looking. The twins were fine. He led her swiftly off the path and pulled her behind a tree, put his hands to her shoulders.

'I've been trying to keep them away from you on purpose.'

'I'm no good for them anyway.'

She scanned his eyes as if she was looking for him to agree with her. The colour around her pupils pulsed in the sun, from sunflower and amber to mahogany. Her sadness was palpable.

His instincts shot to red alert. 'That's just not true, Lucie…'

'Well, I'm not exactly a great role model, am I?' she scoffed self-deprecatingly.

He faltered, tilting her chin up to face him. This wasn't anything he'd heard from her before.

'Not that I'm asking you to fill a role—you know that. But…' An instinctive need to reassure her rose up to his throat. 'But why would you say that?'

'I don't know. I just can't forget how I was—maybe how I still am—because of what happened to Mum and Dad. I missed them so much, and I felt bad about bringing all my drama into Gramma and Grampa's lives—and yours, AJ… And now I'm back here, bringing everything that happened to me in Nepal. The twins must pick up on the fact that I'm not exactly normal…'

He ignored her. 'What drama did you bring to Gramma May? Lucie, she adores you—and so did Bert.'

She chewed on her lip. 'Grampa had to work a lot longer than he should have—for *my* sake,' she said. 'And then he died too soon. Without going with Gramma to see the pyramids of Egypt, or Niagara Falls, or the Great Barrier Reef, or any of the other places they'd planned to go when he retired.'

This was tough to hear. He couldn't help feeling that, for all the years he thought he'd known her, he hadn't actually known much at all.

'They loved you,' he reiterated.

'I know. But it doesn't change the fact that I took something away from them, AJ. And they never talked about my parents with me—ever.'

'Probably because they didn't want you to live in the past, Lucie. They wanted to give you a future. And maybe they were grieving themselves. May loves you so much you don't even know...'

He trailed off. This was not the time to tell her how upset May had been after she'd gone back to the States. But of course the sweet woman hadn't wanted to stand in Lucie's way.

'She told everyone how much she missed you, Luce. *Everyone* here missed you.'

She bit on her lip, as if she hadn't ever thought about that before. 'Well... I felt I had to take Aunt Lina up on her offer,' she said. 'For various reasons.'

He felt his jaw start to twitch. One of those reasons was because of what she thought had happened with him and Claire. If only he'd left his stupid bedroom door open that night, instead of letting Claire close it, he would've seen Lucie appear.

'And it was great,' she continued. 'But Lina wasn't exactly around a lot. She was too independent to change. I guess what I'm saying is, I have no idea how to be a role model for anyone.'

He almost laughed. 'And you think *I* do?'

She winced. 'You're doing so well, AJ. You're the kind of dad who wears out skipping ropes!'

If only she knew the struggles...

'I make it up as I go along, Luce. Trust me—everyone does. Anyway, it's not that I don't want them around you. They love you. I just don't want them to have to miss you.'

He paused as she turned her hands in his, as if she was memorising the feel of them for later. He almost said, *And I don't want to miss you again.* Which was the truth.

But she knew that already. He'd made love to her, hadn't he? He didn't have to say he loved her for her to know...and why should he tell her? She'd only throw his vulnerability right back in his face, then close the door on it again.

He leaned into her, stroked the hair back behind her ears. She narrowed her gaze at the ground as he traced her cheekbone with his thumb, moving it down to her lips. Before he could refrain, he pressed his lips gently to hers. Right now his own feelings didn't matter. He only wanted to kiss away whatever imagined incompetence she might be feeling—no thanks to what she'd gone through as a child.

'I guess all that affected you more than I ever knew—losing your parents, having to move all the way to England, to Yorkshire,' he said, putting a palm to her face.

She leaned into him and he caressed her warm

face, forgetting that he shouldn't. It was only just dawning on him: *this* was why Lucie never felt like anywhere in particular was home.

Lucie urged him closer, pulling him by the collar, and kissed him just as softly, then harder. Every thought flew out of the window and it was no one else but them, just like it had been at his house, in his bedroom…

All too soon she pulled away gently, shaking her head. He resisted emitting the growl of frustration building up in his throat. He'd walked right into that.

Why do you keep doing this to yourself, man?

'Gramma May told me not to mess with your heart,' she told him, pressing her fingers to her lips.

He was silent, thoughts reeling. 'I'm sure she did.'

'I have to go back to my job, AJ.'

Austin shoved his hands through his hair so as not to reach for her again. His heart was already hers, whatever she did—sucker that he was. But moving on was ingrained into Lucie. As for him… He was only just getting used to the thought of loving someone after Ebby. Still trying not to feel awful for even *wanting* to love Lucie.

'Do you know when you're going, exactly?' he managed, thinking of Ruby's and Josiah's faces when he told them Lucie wouldn't be around any more.

'I don't know the exact date yet.'

He bit his tongue as they walked back to the path. Asking her to stay wouldn't work. If he kept pushing he'd only push her further away—like last time. And what did he have to offer a global wanderer anyway, except chains?

Maple's sudden barks were manic, deafening.

'What's up, girl?'

Lucie reached out to pat her, but Maple ran halfway back towards the group, stopped, and then ran back to them, wagging her tail furiously.

He and Lucie exchanged glances.

'She's acting strangely…' Austin scanned the path ahead, then Lucie's face. She was on high alert now, as he was.

'This happened before…when John had his seizure,' she said, clutching his arm.

Just then Jetson bounded back to them and started barking wildly too. His stomach dropped. Then they both hit the ground running.

CHAPTER TWENTY-ONE

THEY REACHED Tom just in time to stop his head from crashing into the ground.

'He's having a heart attack!'

Lucie's heart bucked in her chest as she lowered him down, cushioning his fall.

Austin, already on the phone, went straight for the twins. He guided them to the side of the path before joining her, and they watched, wide-eyed, as she and their dad knelt beside the ashen-faced man on the ground.

His pale cream trousers were streaked with mud where he'd fallen. He must be…what? Sixty? She swallowed the panic that was building in her at the sight of him, clutching his chest in the middle of the forest.

Focus.

How far had they walked from the car park already?

'I'm a doctor,' Lucie said, clearing the bystanders with one quick command.

The dogs barked and yapped wildly, even as

people tried to calm them. Had the dogs really tried to warn them again, *before* this had even happened? Jetson was the one who'd spurred AJ into action, but Maple had seemed to know something was up, too.

'It feels like a ten-ton bear is sitting on my chest,' the man croaked.

Discomfort was etched into every line of his face, but he was conscious.

'OK, Tom...' Lucie placed a hand on the man's arm comfortingly, while AJ finished the call he was making to the emergency services. 'When did this start?'

'Just a few minutes ago. I thought it must be heartburn...' He tailed off, wincing, then dropped in her arms.

'His eyes are closing,' she whispered, laying the man down as gently as she could.

He was groaning now, drawing deep, ghastly breaths, as if the atmosphere had been sucked from all around him. 'He's definitely in cardiac arrest.'

AJ was right there, looking to her for guidance. 'What can I do?'

'Help me,' she ordered, unbuttoning his shirt.

The twins were mumbling in panic by the trees, along with the rest of their group. Somewhere, someone was sobbing. The dogs whimpered intermittently, in a spooky soundtrack.

'Stay with us...help is coming,' she told Tom, as AJ used his own jacket as a pillow.

Pressing her hands to his heart, she thought Tom's skin felt strangely cold. His face turned an even whiter shade of pale and he drooped some more. She started chest compressions.

Please, please, please...

AJ's hand on her back told her when to stop. She let him take over the next round, letting his confidence calm her. The knees of his jeans were caked in dirt, but AJ's face showed pure, fierce determination.

'Come on, Tom!'

Lucie cast her eyes to the twins, who were sobbing now, and in the distance she heard sirens wail.

Moments later two paramedics appeared, and AJ half stumbled backwards into her, letting them take over.

'He's breathing—let's get him up!'

The twins rocketed into them both, almost sending them tumbling to the floor as Tom was given an oxygen mask and loaded onto the stretcher.

'Daddy! You saved his life!'

Ruby's face was streaked with tears, and Lucie had only just composed her thoughts when Josiah threw his arms around her middle and hung on tight.

'Lucie saved him, too,' he said loudly, as if this was his proudest moment to date.

He squeezed her so hard with his little arms that he jolted a nervous laugh from her, and in seconds

Ruby was hugging her as well, fighting to get more of her in her grasp than her brother.

Jetson and Maple jumped at them too, eager to get in on the attention.

AJ ruffled their hair, thanked Jetson, and as the paramedics hurried off the way they'd come with Tom she realised the crowd of walkers and several other passers-by were clapping and cheering them.

She closed her eyes, feeling awkward and embarrassed. This wasn't what she needed or expected. She'd just been in the right place at the right time…and if it hadn't been for the dogs they might not have got to Tom in time to stop serious injury—he might have been hurt if he'd fallen.

AJ's arm snaked around her. Silencing her thoughts in one fell swoop, he pulled her harder into their group hug. Lucie let her relief and gratitude out into his broad chest, breathing in his comforting scent as her heartrate slowed.

Her face finally broke into a smile, although she was half expecting the squeeze of an enthusiastic child to bring her to her knees.

'Jetson tried to warn us,' AJ said later when, exhausted and hungry, they took the twins back to the house for sandwiches. 'Maple, too.'

Lucie sat back in the couch. 'I know.'

Accepting the glass of water he'd poured her, she looked for signs of distress in Ruby and Josiah, who were busy making the dogs their dinner.

'I was thinking that. Do you think she's learning from Jetson without even being trained?'

He shrugged thoughtfully. 'Interesting concept. There's so much more research to be done,' he said, brushing down his jeans.

They were still streaked with mud. She pictured the shower upstairs. They shouldn't… The twins were here. They couldn't. Not that she would have anyway, she reminded herself. Gramma had told her not to mess with his heart, and hers had been messed with enough, too.

But, then again, he was the one who'd kissed her back there. *Again.*

'Daddy, when we sell the house, can Jetson still live with us?'

Lucie drew her lips together.

Visibly thrown, AJ sank to the couch beside her, a wall of tension all over again. Her hand found his in support—she couldn't help it.

'Who told you we're selling the house, Rubes?'

Ruby had refused to let Lucie go back to her own house this evening and, all things considered, Lucie had relented. No kid should have to see what they'd watched playing out today. Surprisingly, though, they seemed fine, obsessing on Lucie and AJ being heroes, rather than the tragedy itself. Till now.

Ruby eyed her father beguilingly from her place on the carpet, where she was now brushing Jetson. 'I heard you and Auntie Belle talking about it.'

'We'll talk about it later Ruby-Roo,' he said gently, looking down at Lucie's hand in his before removing it gently.

Lucie cringed inside.

Josiah had wandered in. He plonked a book called *Aliens and the Mysteries of the Universe* onto Lucie's lap. 'What are you talking about?'

'Daddy's selling the house,' Ruby informed him. 'I was asking if Jetson can still live with us.'

Josiah's face fell. 'But where will we go?'

To Lucie's horror, his eyes pooled with tears. Impulsively she drew an arm around him, held him tight.

AJ looked drained.

'Nothing's been decided yet, sweetie,' she said on his behalf, as soothingly as she could, willing AJ to turn around and face them.

Suddenly she was nine years old again herself, being told she had to leave Colorado for a place in England called Brookborough. Lost. Frightened.

AJ stood and paced the living room, stopping by the window. Ruby continued brushing Jetson pensively.

'We can't stay here for ever, guys,' he said with a sigh.

'Why not?' Josiah demanded, through a sob and a sniff.

'We just can't.'

Lucie drummed her hand on her knee. 'Nothing has been decided yet,' she said again, racking her brains for a way she could make this situation better. No child should ever feel forced out of their home.

AJ's shoulders tensed. He eyed her arm around Josiah until she felt as though she shouldn't have hugged him.

'We have to be realistic. Auntie Belle is moving out. It's too big for just us three.'

'Not if Lucie moves in,' Ruby said, matter-of-factly.

Josiah nodded vehemently, wiping at his tears. The look of hope on his face sent her reeling.

'Yes! Lucie can move in! And Maple.'

Lucie scratched at her neck, avoiding AJ's eyes. Kids said the craziest things…but it seemed AJ had been right. For some reason she would never understand, they did really seem to like her.

'Lucie's not staying,' AJ said sternly.

OK…

The seriousness on his face spoke a thousand words. The twins wanting her around was everything he didn't want to happen, and after their conversation earlier it was hardly surprising he'd decided to tell them the truth. She'd pretty much hammered it home that she was definitely going back to work abroad.

So why did she feel so sick?

Because you told him Gramma May warned you not to mess with his heart and he said nothing. His heart seems perfectly fine!

Ruby pouted. 'Where are you going, Lucie?'

'I don't know yet, honey,' she answered.

She was thinking of the bookmark, the memorial book that was waiting for her in Peru. Maybe she'd go to Cusco, to the base there, while she waited for her next position.

Ruby's blue eyes were narrowed in genuine confusion. 'If you don't know where you're going, how will you know when you get there?'

Silence.

Lucie opened her mouth to reply, but a snort of laughter from Josiah cut her off. Then Ruby started giggling, till both children were rolling on the floor with the dogs, laughing hysterically, as if she'd proposed the riddle to end all riddles.

Her mouth twitched in amusement. Kids were insane.

AJ rolled his eyes and dropped back to the couch. 'Welcome to my world,' he sighed, so close to her it made her ear tickle in anticipation.

Today had been crazy, totally unexpected on all accounts, but at least they were laughing. The subject of the house going up for sale was dismissed, at least for now, and she was here. She shouldn't be. But she was. And the rare moment of togetherness curled and swirled inside her, warming her blood.

Yawning, she moved to lean her head against AJ's shoulder.

He stiffened.

Before she'd even touched his shirt he jumped to his feet again, held his hand out to her. 'I'll walk you to the door.'

'Oh, yes…thanks,' she said quickly, as if she'd been about to leave anyway.

Gosh, how mortifying… But what did she expect?

'Say goodbye to Lucie, kids,' AJ told them, and they obliged—but not before Josiah asked for a bedtime story.

Flustered, she told him, 'Not tonight, sweetie.'

At the door, AJ looked at her apologetically.

'You don't have to say it,' she told him, pulling on her jacket. 'I understand.'

'It's just… I can't do it to them, Lucie,' he said. 'Selling the house, you leaving—it's all a lot for them.'

'And for you too?' she said, searching his face.'

He straightened up. A flicker of anger crossed his features. When he spoke, his voice was tight. 'I'll see you before you leave?'

She pursed her lips, ignoring the way he was drawing a line under her imminent departure already. So he wasn't going to talk about the truth of it. That no matter what he said, and whether she left or not, she could never give him half of what Ebby had.

'I guess so,' she said.

He nodded, and lingered for a moment, watching her in a way that made her wish she could read his mind the way she'd always used to feel she could.

'Lucie, thank you for today. You were...' He tailed off, scratched his chin, and she forced a straight face.

Awkward.

She turned around, forcing herself not to look back. She knew he was watching her walk away, and she could literally feel him observing the space between them widening.

CHAPTER TWENTY-TWO

NIGEL REACHED OVER to Lucie from behind a box of bananas, offered her a high five over the market stall, then tossed her an orange.

'Great job Miss Henderson,' he said, throwing a wink at Gramma May, who was inspecting the avocados.

Lucie racked her brains.

'Tom,' Nigel reminded her. 'You and Austin saved that guy from kicking the bucket in the woods. Thank God you were there, yeah? He's a good friend of my wife's sister…runs the model train shop?'

Lucie smiled awkwardly as Gramma May handed Nigel an avocado and some grapes to weigh. No end of people had cornered her over the last week or so, telling her how they all knew Tom, thanking her as if she was their new hero. A reporter had even called the day after it had happened and asked to interview her.

She'd politely declined. She was no hero. If only they knew!

'You've got a good one here, May,' Nigel said, dropping the fruit into a paper bag. 'Do we know if we can keep her yet?'

Lucie cringed, and then told him her locum position was almost up and she'd be leaving soon—which was starting to sound scary even to her own ears. An email from her team had arrived only that morning, and was still sitting unanswered in her inbox. She had drafted a reply, deleted the draft, retyped it and deleted it again more times than she could count.

There was more flooding in Pakistan. Landslides. Buried villages. The team were congregating in Karachi ASAP. They wanted to know if she would join them. Her hotel room would be ready for her, they said.

Guilt raged through her. She'd let her feelings for AJ get in the way of all her promises, but time was quickly ticking down on her now.

Usually she'd have been chomping at the bit to get back out there, but this place and its people had sneaked their way into her heart and tugged at her ventricles like vines. And AJ... All she could think about was him. The way they'd left things, all weird and unfinished.

That was what it was. Unfinished. They'd always be unfinished.

But he hadn't given her any indication at all that he wanted her to stay for anything other than her job as a locum and her friendship.

Maple was waiting patiently for scraps by the fish stand up ahead, but before she could make her way over Gramma May's excited cry echoed Nigel's.

'Pamela!'

AJ's mother.

Lucie froze.

'I didn't know you were visiting from Naples,' May enthused, dropping a kiss to her cheek.

The two women started chattering at a million miles an hour, and then Pamela's eyes shot to her. A warm smile that looked so much like AJ's spread from ear to ear as she held both hands out.

'My Lucie-Lu. Oh, pet, it's so good to see you!'

Pamela made a fuss of her, told her how lovely she looked, told her how Doug, AJ's dad, had been asking after her. It was a flood of love. Lucie was moved.

Before she quite knew how to put her head up out of the whirlwind, she'd accepted an invitation for dinner on Friday at the house they were renting for the week in Whitby.

Austin had been catching the pretty research assistant's eyes on him all morning. *Annabel*, according to her name tag. Blonde, blue-eyed…the kind of young, pretty thing he would have gone for before Ebby, probably.

The opposite of Lucie.

'They got it again, Austin,' she said now in excitement, hurrying over to him and patting the golden Retriever, the Labrador and the border collie on her way. 'They all identified the contaminated samples over the clean ones. That's four different bacteria types with over ninety percent accuracy!'

'I had every faith they would,' he said, as his volunteers whispered excitedly amongst themselves and praised their dogs.

This was just one part of the disease detection training they'd been perfecting here at the hospital, in a dedicated research space, getting the dogs to sniff out urinary tract infections from female urine samples. Not the most glamorous of tasks, but still important.

He was going over his notes with Annabel, her warm breath tickling his cheek, when there was a knock at the door. He saw Lucie peering through the glass before she stepped inside, and something made him take a step back from Annabel. But not before he'd caught the look of jealousy in Lucie's expression.

'Hi!' he said, surprised to see her.

'Hi,' she said. 'I thought you'd still be here.'

Her eyes darted to Annabel and he introduced them quickly, not missing the way Lucie looked her up and down as if she was sizing up a rival boxer in a ring. There it was again—the green-eyed monster. Something about seeing it in Lucie tickled him…

'I brought Constance to say hello,' Lucie said now, motioning for her to step in from the corridor. 'We were just running a check-up on her.'

Constance beamed as she took his hand with both of hers, then reached for Annabel's—which seemed to irk Lucie more.

'I got the all-clear,' Constance told them.

'Oh, that's great news,' he said, relieved.

Lucie nodded. 'The biopsy came back clean for cancer cells,' she told him, looking to Annabel again, who still kind of hovered, like she had been all morning. 'Now it's just a check-up every six months and a colonoscopy every few years to make sure no more tumours sneak back in. But we're hoping that's it.'

Constance smoothed down her silk scarf. She already looked less gaunt, and her face had more colour. 'Thank goodness. I mean, I'm still a little weak post-surgery, but I still can't thank you and these dogs enough, Dr Johnstone. Because of them I'm alive.'

'Yes, you are.' He smiled. 'And you'll be happy to know we've just been approved to showcase the new disease detection course at the Global Medicine Conference in Chicago next month. Thera Pups is expanding faster than I could have anticipated.'

'That's so wonderful,' the women chorused, and Annabel clapped her hands together in agreement.

Austin saw Lucie flinch. Was she sad that she wouldn't be around to see it grow on home turf?

Lucie cleared her throat as Annabel touched his arm lightly, drawing his attention back to her. 'I'll be outside, I have some calls to make,' she said, speaking a little too close to his ear. 'Nice to meet you both.'

Lucie's lips were a thin, cross line. Her eyes burned into him. He raised his eyebrows at her as Annabel slipped out. It wasn't his fault if women flirted with him. In fact, he usually barely noticed them doing it. But Lucie had woken something up inside him. Some kind of hormone that spoke on his behalf about craving…wanting…needing.

It was Lucie he craved, obviously—for all the good it was doing him. They'd only seen each other a handful of times since he'd escorted her out of the house, mostly just in passing at the hospital. Watching her go that day, all he'd wanted was to run after her and kiss her, stick his last flag in the sand as a claim on what was his before it flew out of reach. But what good would that have done? Besides, he had to put the kids and their feelings first.

Constance had just bade them both farewell, and he was about to excuse himself from Lucie too, when his phone pinged with a message from his mum.

Is Lucie still a vegetarian? I don't have her number, sorry!

'Has my mother invited you to dinner on Friday as well?' he asked her, as he led her outside into the corridor.

Annabel was on the phone across the hall, but she held her hand up at him in a wave, which he returned—much to Lucie's obvious annoyance.

'You're coming too?' Lucie crossed her arms warily, then moved to block Annabel from his eyeline. 'I thought it was a personal invitation for me and Gramma.'

He blew air through his lips. Of course he was going too. The twins were coming with him. They couldn't get enough of their grandparents whenever they flew over to visit.

'Mum and Dad don't know anything,' he told her now.

Lucie's eyes narrowed. 'What do you mean?'

'About us,' he said, lowering his voice and picturing their faces if he told them how he'd put the twins' happiness in jeopardy all over again, giving them false hope about Lucie sticking around.

Talk about bad parenting.

'There is no us,' she retorted.

Ouch.

'Anyway, do you really think no one's told them about the pond incident?'

He frowned. She had a point. If they didn't know yet, they soon would.

'I'll just tell them something's come up and I can't go, if that's what you think is best,' she offered, glancing at Annabel again.

Austin considered it. The last thing they needed was any drama around the dinner table. Lucie would have to explain yet again that she didn't know where she was going next, and he'd have to bite his damn tongue to stop making a fool of himself, begging her once more not to put her life in danger. As if he had any claim on her, really.

Why did his parents have to ask her to dinner? 'AJ?'

The hurt in her eyes caught him off guard. Maybe he was being a little selfish. She'd used to be pretty close to his mother, who'd always adored her.

'Do you want me to stay away?'

'No, don't be silly—you should come,' he said on a sigh. 'Mum's asking if you're still a vegetarian, by the way.'

'I forgot about that phase.'

She laughed dully, but her heart clearly wasn't in it. She seemed distracted now. Was she thinking about Annabel? Wondering if anything was going on?

So what if she is? She isn't sticking around. This will be both a hello and a goodbye dinner, as far as Mum and Dad are concerned.

'I'll see you on Friday, then? I'll pick you up and we can drive there together.' Even as the words came out, he kicked himself. 'It makes sense… just taking one car. You, me, Gramma May and the twins,' he reasoned aloud.

'I guess so,' she replied.

But he caught the uncertainty in her eyes, and one final glare in Annabel's direction too, before she turned and left.

CHAPTER TWENTY-THREE

THE DRIVE BACK from her last home visit felt as if it took for ever. Lucie only half saw the beauty she was starting to take for granted again. The open pastures with their horses…the endless trees and huge brown barns. Her head kept flitting to tonight's dinner and whether she should actually go.

AJ had been flirting *so* hard the other day at the hospital…or at least that pretty blonde research assistant, Annabel, had been flirting with him. Lucie half expected to find her sitting at the dinner table tonight, engrossed in conversation with Pamela and Doug.

AJ hadn't been in touch at all since they'd discussed whether she should go or not. Maybe he really didn't want her to come and was hoping she would cancel.

She scowled at a scarecrow in a field as she passed it. He was probably wishing she'd already left, so he could just get on with asking Annabel out—and all the other women who'd fall for him after just one scan of his online dating profile.

Yuck.

Flicking the radio on to calm the fresh wave of jealousy that was strangling her brain, she heard another news bulletin blast through the car. The floods in Pakistan were getting worse. She had no real reason to be here, she reminded herself. Her locum position would be pretty much all wrapped up in a matter of days, when the full-time doctor returned.

She'd done the right thing the other day, finally replying to the email that she'd been stewing over. So what if her jealousy over AJ and Annabel's flirting had been the final catalyst? She would've had to do it anyway…she'd just been stalling.

She hadn't told him yet, though. The thought sent a bolt of dread through her innards every time.

The second she'd hit 'send', and confirmed she'd be joining them shortly, a scroll had gone across her brain with the words *Just tell him* on it. She'd picked up her phone, let her finger hover over his name. It would not swipe. It simply would not let her call him.

The thought of it made her feel quite nauseous. The fact that she'd sent the email at all had set some kind of slow-release hand grenade in motion. She'd opened the email up in the 'sent' folder, re-read the confidence with which she'd written her reply, trying to make the firm decision sound real. It hadn't really worked. The confidence had been faked to begin with.

She would have to tell AJ now. So he could pre-pare…if he still cared.

What if he *didn't* care, thought? Oh, God. Hearing the indifference in his voice would be heartbreaking, to say the least. She'd sit on the plane, imagining him out on a date, laughing about little lost Lucie with Annabel…

Oh, stop feeling sorry for yourself, she scorned herself, pulling up at some lights.

It really couldn't wait much longer. Time was ticking.

Her hand lingered over her phone, in its holder on the dashboard. She had to tell him.

Now?

No, she decided, chickening out again. Tonight, after dinner.

Austin stepped out of the car outside Gramma May's, checking himself in the wing mirror. His nerves were shot.

'Hey,' he said, when Lucie opened the door.

She smoothed down her maroon dress and he vaguely registered that the colour of it matched his sweater, as if they'd planned it. Of course, she would look stunning.

Maple greeted him, then sprinted past him to the car, where Jetson was waiting.

'No Gramma May?' he asked, looking over her shoulder.

'She said she'd meet us there. She went shopping in Whitby,' she said.

'OK. Well, the twins are already with Mum and Dad—they picked them up after school.'

Lucie looked flustered, as if she had something on her mind. More than just their impending awkward ride for two to Whitby. It fed his own anxiety. Her time was up at the surgery—just a few more days next week, as a crossover to fill the doctor in, and then she'd be free. But he didn't think she'd booked a flight anywhere yet. She would have told him.

'Shall we go?' he said, touching a hand to her back as she took the steps down from the door.

He held the car door open for her. Maple jumped in first, of course, and the small space closed in on them in the twilight. He'd wrestled with the urge to ask her to stay so many times, just as he wanted to do now, the second he had her to himself... But every time that voice in his head told him he was crazy. She wanted to get back to her adventures. She was only passing through. This was probably the last time he'd drive her anywhere.

'Oh, shoot,' she said suddenly, just as he'd started the ignition. 'The pie! Gramma asked me to bring an apple pie for dessert, and it's on the kitchen counter.'

'Stay with the dogs. I'll run in,' he told her, cutting the engine and taking the door keys from her hands.

In moments he was standing in the cinnamon-scented kitchen. The darkened room was lit only by the screen of a laptop. He recognised it. Lucie's.

Where was the pie...?

He picked it up from the counter, glanced at the laptop again to check the time—Pamela hated it when people were late and her appetisers went cold.

An email was open on the screen. Clutching the pie to his chest, he couldn't help catch the subject line.

Karachi assignment accepted.

Leaning in closer, he read some more. His blood ran cold.

He left the pie where it was and stormed back outside to confront her, fury and humiliation making a storm of his entire mind. She'd arranged all *this* without telling him.

'I'm sorry, AJ,' Lucie said, her eyes wide with shock and guilt. 'I know I should have told you sooner.'

'I can't believe you.'

He turned to her as she scrambled out of the car. Her shoes clicked on the tarmac and the breeze picked up her dress.

'When were you going to tell me?'

'You always knew I was leaving, AJ. The locum position was only for—'

He shook his head. 'I asked you recently for an *exact* date.'

She shrugged. 'I didn't know it till now.'

'You've known for days that you're going to Pakistan and you've made all the arrangements—it was all in the email!'

She reached for his hands, but he pulled them back. 'AJ, look, I just didn't know how to tell you...'

'It's pretty simple, Lucie. You just say it!' he seethed, as the memories crashed back over him of the last time he'd discovered she'd skipped town, with no word to him about why, or where she was going. 'This isn't much better than last time, when you got on that plane and left for America without warning!'

She shook her head, dropped to sit on the stone wall. 'You know why I have to go this time.'

Humiliation clouded his brain. Some part of him knew he didn't really have the right to be this angry with her, that this had always been going to happen. It was why he'd tried to keep his distance in the first place.

If only he hadn't bombed at it.

For a second words hovered on his lips...the truth.

I love you...don't go again. Don't leave me wondering if you're dead or alive. You are all I want.

I would even have chosen you over Ebby if you hadn't left the first time, and the guilt of that's nearly been killing me!

He stopped himself, as if frozen in time, staring at her face. He barely recognised her now. She would seriously just up and leave him all over again? After everything they'd shared? She'd known when she was going, and the fact she hadn't told him... Did she really care that little about him?

'AJ, please...'

She reached for him again but he pulled away, turned for the car. He was already picturing the floodwaters in Pakistan... Lucie losing her footing on some mud bank, sliding away in a monsoon.

Ebby was gone. He'd stomped all over her memory for Lucie. And now he was going to have neither of them.

She followed him to the car, then stopped as he yanked it open. The dogs were whining. 'Are we really going to leave it like this?'

He couldn't even respond. The last time he'd seen Ebby he'd been too distracted at the prospect of staying at home alone with their twin babies even to kiss her goodbye. It had never crossed his mind that it could all just end like that...that she wouldn't ever come home again.

Now it was all he could think about. Him waving Lucie off and waiting. Waiting for the news.

She opened her mouth to speak, but he wouldn't

hear her—not one more word that would only haunt him for the rest of his life.

'Just go,' he spat. 'Go! Go and be a hero. But if you do, don't come back here. Because I don't want to see you again. And I don't want my kids to see you either.'

I don't want to have to think about you dying out there.

'AJ...'

'I mean it, Lucie.'

A strange sense of déjà vu settled over him as she pressed her hands to her eyes.

'I never should have made love to you,' he heard himself growl, and Lucie's sobs broke his heart in two.

He sat heavily in the driver's seat, slammed the door and skidded away so hard he knew the asphalt would carry the scars for months.

So what? The separation process started now. This second. On *his* terms this time.

CHAPTER TWENTY-FOUR

LUCIE PRESSED HERSELF against the wall in the busy hotel reception area. The signal here in Karachi was less than reliable for reaching Yorkshire, but Gramma May was asking about Maple's costume for the Paws Under the Stars event. It was happening just one week from now. She'd never felt so far away from where her heart ached to be.

With the costume located, in a bag in the wardrobe, Lucie waved to a passing colleague as Gramma May told her Maple had learned some new tricks under her care, which made her heart swell. Gramma loved the dog so much that she'd adopted her. It was hard not to miss them both.

AJ's words were still a hideous echo in her head.

'I don't want to see you again. And I don't want my kids to see you either.'

'So, where is it you're flying to the day after to-morrow?' Gramma May asked.

'Another of the flood zones,' Lucie said, relaying the name of a village she could barely pronounce, straining to be heard over a Tannoy announcement and a rumbling trolley packed with towels.

She was exhausted already. She and the team had flown to three rural locations and back to their new base here on the outskirts of Karachi over the past two weeks. Keeping busy was key. She'd poured her heart and soul into it—counselling homeless women and kids at schools and community centres, making sure the local dogs were fed.

But AJ was everywhere.

He never left her head.

She was itching to ask Gramma May about him, but no. There was absolutely no point. Instead she let Gramma tell her about Nigel's new market stall cat, and asked about Tom, who was now back in his model train shop, seemingly fit and healthy. Thinking about all the people she'd grown so fond of made her smile.

Then Gramma said, 'Austin's house is on the market. I reckon it'll sell pretty fast.'

Lucie's stomach lurched. She forced a wave at another passing colleague, turned to the wall. So surreal…

'Did you hear me?'

'Uh-huh,' she said, wiping at her face.

It was hot here. Too hot. Uncomfortable in more ways than one. Tiredness was making her bones ache. And the dreams had found her again. Not about floods or earthquakes. Those were over.

The nightmares were different now. They were all about AJ shutting doors, calling from the other side of walls. And the worst one…him passionately kissing Annabel, right in front of her.

Somehow, since she'd left and put all this physical space between them, he'd become absorbed even deeper into her bloodstream. He'd felt like home. And now she was here, and everything felt wrong, and they weren't even speaking.

She growled in exasperation. '*Ugh*… I made a mess of things, didn't I, Gramma? You warned me not to hurt him and I did.'

Gramma was silent for a moment. 'I think you're hurting each other,' she said. 'Am I allowed to speak about him this time?'

Lucie frowned as her heart bashed her ribcage. 'Yes,' she managed, dreading what she might hear. 'But please don't tell me you've seen his dating profile, Gramma.'

'I don't think he wants to date anyone, Lucie.'

She felt sick. 'Yes, he does.'

'He's worried to death that you'll die out there, Lucie! For God's sake, can't you see that?'

Lucie clutched at her stomach, sliding down the wall to the floor.

'He doesn't *want* to love you in case something happens to you—like it did to Ebby.'

Lucie pressed a hand to the phone to hide her sniffle. Gramma sounded so distressed.

'He's already lost you once, Lucie, can you blame him for shutting down? God knows, we all missed you enough the first time, so please...just come home.'

Tears ran down Lucie's face. 'I didn't think you'd miss me very much the first time, Gramma. Not after what I did.'

Gramma was silent a moment. Then, 'What you did?'

Lucie swallowed. 'I forced Grampa to go back to work, so you could afford to care for me. I made you stop living your life after he died. You should have gone travelling, seen the world...'

'Honestly, where is all this coming from? I've done plenty of trips with Cynthia, and we're perfectly fine. I've seen enough of the world through you and your eyes, too. My darling, in no way did you force anyone to do anything—we did it all with love. Grampa wouldn't have swapped raising you for all the pyramids in Egypt!'

Gramma May went on to reassure her that Grampa's early death had been in no way her fault. He'd always kept his dodgy heart a secret. They laughed about the memories they had of him, and cried about a few more. She'd never felt this close to Gramma May, ever, and yet so far away at the same time.

Lucie was so moved and so exhausted when she hung up that she wept on the floor until a passing stranger had to hand her a tissue.

* * *

Hours later, she was still processing Gramma's words, alone in a tiny, dimly lit restaurant that had none of the charm of Brookborough's Old Ram Inn. AJ didn't want to love her in case he lost her. He might feel terrible for having moved on from Ebby with her—but he did love her, and he was hurting now she'd left.

She cursed her own idiocy and her stubborn pride, picturing Ruby and Josiah. There wasn't a day that dawned when she didn't think of them and how they'd bonded, against all the odds. No wonder AJ had tried to keep her away from the twins…from himself. He'd been protecting himself and them from another disaster.

A stray dog loitered at the restaurant door. She stood up with some scraps of meat she'd saved, making a new friend in an instant. The dog walked her back to the hotel, and she fought tears the whole way.

It was almost ironic, how much of a disaster she was. She'd given it a good shot, but AJ was right. All this stupid guilt had piled up on her. Guilt for shutting out what was left of her family, and for living her life when Jorge had lost his.

But that guilt was no good to anyone! Her heart was at home, where she was loved unconditionally.

'How could I have been so stupid?' she said to the dog.

Maybe it wasn't too late.

* * *

Austin stood in the corner of the kitchen, watching the couple opening his cupboards, taking measurements along his windowsills. It was so strange, watching other people planning a life in his home.

Belle saw the look on his face and took him aside. 'You don't have to do this, you know,' she whispered. 'Nothing's been signed yet.'

'It's fine, Belle,' he said, forcing himself to believe it.

Belle wasn't buying it. She stepped backwards onto a stray plastic puzzle piece and her yelp made the couple turn in surprise.

One of them mumbled something like, 'Thank God we won't have kids in this house!' and they chuckled between them.

Belle looked infuriated. 'It's not fine, Austin, it's wrong,' she hissed. 'Lucie should be here with you. You both love this house and you love each other! I don't know how this has gone so wrong.' Belle hopped around the hallway, holding her foot. 'You had the girl of your dreams right here and you let her go. Again!'

'Don't make a scene,' he told his sister quietly.

She didn't know about the open ticket to Karachi, burning a hole through his drawer upstairs, but she was right. He had let Lucie go. He'd practically ordered her away from him and now nothing made much sense any more.

But…

There was always a but.

'It's been five years, AJ!' Belle simmered, kicking the puzzle piece out of view under the stairs. 'Are you seriously still telling yourself you're not supposed to be moving on? Ebby would want you to be happy, you know!'

Austin dropped to the bottom step of the stairs, his eyes on the couple who were now making a wide circle around Jetson as if he might suddenly attack them, or eat the shoes from their feet. They clearly weren't fans of dogs, either.

He scrubbed at his face. Regret and shame had coated his bones since the second he'd sped from that driveway, and it wasn't just Belle reminding him of his glaring faults lately. Everyone in this village had hammered it home over the past few weeks, in their own special ways.

'Where's Lucie? We love Lucie.'

'Lucie is one of those rare special ones, pet.'

'Oh? What do you mean she's left again already?'

In his head he'd boarded that plane a thousand times already, followed Gramma May's instructions to find the hotel in Karachi, told Lucie everything that had stopped him begging her not to go when she'd been standing here right in front of him.

But the house sale…the kids…his patients…

What if you get there and she still doesn't want to come home?

The woman in the pea-green coat dragged a finger along the top of the fridge. She grimaced at what she saw, and then she moved Ruby's dog drawing from under its alphabet magnet, where it had been for three whole years.

It was the final straw. He was losing his mind. This house was his, and it had always been Lucie's too.

Family.

He hadn't tried hard enough before to keep her here. But this time…

'Belle,' he said, interrupting her mid-rant, 'can you please look after the twins till I get back?'

'Wait—what? Where are you going?' she called out in confusion.

He was already sprinting up the stairs.

CHAPTER TWENTY-FIVE

LUCIE WHEELED HER bags out of the elevator into the bright hotel reception area, clutching the giant memorial book. Jorge's widow had done his memory proud. Her colleagues had flown it out here to Karachi for her. She just prayed it wasn't too big for her carry-on.

It was raining outside. Would she even be able to get a taxi to the airport at this hour?

Now that she'd made her mind up, and her team had been informed that she was leaving, she'd expected a sense of excitement to find its way to her. It hadn't reached her yet. All she felt was nerves.

What if she got all the way back to Brookborough and AJ still didn't want to see her?

At least she would know she'd tried, she supposed. At least she wouldn't have let her panic over another rejection stand in the way of what she really wanted.

Maybe she'd imagined most of it, all these years. People hadn't always left her out in the cold... If anything, she'd been the one to leave them.

'Taxi, please?' she asked the receptionist.

'Maybe I can drive you. Where are you trying to get to?' came a voice from behind her.

'I'd rather get an official cab, thank you,' she said, flustered, turning around.

A man in a raincoat shoved the hood back from his face.

Lucie dropped the memorial book to the floor with a thud.

Oh, my God.

'AJ…?' She blinked, fully expecting the mirage to melt away into a puddle of rain.

He picked up the book, put it on the counter and took her hands. His blue eyes brimmed with intense regret and determination, and she flung herself straight into his arms.

'What are you doing here?' Her voice came out as a croak as his big arms looped around her, tightly and possessively. She'd never been this glad to see *anyone*.

'I didn't come to get you once before, when I should have. Lucie, you have to forgive me for what I said last time I saw you. I wasn't thinking straight.'

'I can't believe you're here…' It was all she could manage.

His warmth, his familiar smell…he was even wearing the cable knit sweater that made her want to curl up against his chest, where she was safe.

'You came all the way *here*…'

'I know you have to work, and I know it's what you want, but you're in my blood, my Lucie. I couldn't let you go again without telling you how much I love you.'

The receptionist wiped a tear from her eye, and then pretended she wasn't watching and listening to all this.

Lucie pulled Austin down to the couch. 'My God, AJ, this is crazy. I was about to go to the airport...to come home.'

'So you *do* know where home is?'

His voice was pure relief, and her heart skidded as he stroked his thumbs across her hands, then reached for her face again. Lucie melted into his fierce kiss there on the tiny hotel couch. She'd already forgotten completely where she was, or that she'd made possibly the biggest decision of her life without even knowing he was already on his way here.

Gramma must have told him where she was. But he'd made this decision on his own. He wouldn't have done anything like this unless he was one hundred percent serious about wanting her in his life, in the twins' lives.

'I've quit,' she said quietly. 'You were right. I don't need to do this—not full-time anyway. Maybe a few weeks of the year, in some less dangerous places, so you're not worried about me. You could even come with me if you wanted to...' She tailed off and he laughed.

'That I could deal with. But, you know, there's a vital position opening up with Thera Pups and the research clinic. I know people. I could put a word in.'

'They all know me already—no thanks to a certain incident in a pond that almost made the local news.'

He kissed her again, and she scruffed up his damp hair with her hands, thanking whatever god was looking out for her that she hadn't lost him.

'I love you. I don't want you to worry about me leaving you, AJ—ever,' she said quickly. 'I'm not going anywhere. You're my home. And Ruby, and Josiah, and Gramma—all of you.'

'I almost sold the house,' he said, grinning against her forehead. 'But I couldn't do it. The couple hate dogs. And kids, apparently.'

'Well, that's no good!' She laughed, breathing him in...her lifeblood.

Maybe she had met her soulmate when she was nine years old. If only she hadn't just given her room up she'd have dragged him into it.

'It's your house too,' he said, seriously. 'If you want it. With me.'

'I do.' She bit her lip, then kissed him yet again...and again.

She kissed him pretty much all the way home.

Austin glanced around the gleaming gardens. A sense of pride settled on his shoulders along with the late-afternoon sun, just from looking around at his volunteers—and Lucie. She'd been up since seven o'clock that morning, helping him lug boxes of Thera Pups calendars and branded hats and harnesses into their spot in the castle grounds. The Paws Under the Stars event was sold out.

Gilling Castle's gardens were stunning right now, surmounted by carved lions and lined with blossoming flowers. To their credit, the twins had been good as gold all day, running about with their friends. They couldn't wait to see the dogs all lit up later, and to start their stargazing safari.

'The dogs look so great!' Constance squealed, greeting Jetson as he bounded up to her in his costume. 'Is he a hot dog?' she asked, taking in the squishy fabric bread rolls either side of him, and the fake mustard blob tied around his head.

Lucie came up beside him in a long red dress, slipping her hand into his. 'He is. And Maple is... Where is my little Yoda?'

Austin squeezed her hand. Just her being here beside him was still unreal to him. The fact that she'd moved into the house the same night he'd brought her home even more so. Words could not describe how good it had felt...the two of them ripping the *For Sale* sign from the daffodil patch and tossing it onto the bonfire.

He spotted Maple. 'There she is. Maple! Come here, girl!'

Maple padded over from her place with Gramma

May, Flora McNally from the gift shop and Cynthia, who'd kindly donated special dog-shaped sweets from the chocolate shop. *The coven*, he called them. They waved at him from the merchandise stall and brandished the new calendar excitedly.

He put a finger to his lips. Lucie hadn't seen it yet.

The second Maple reached an adoring Constance she was immediately called away again, by young Samuel, who was making Bingo the beagle perform an impressive jump and spin move. Everyone was here.

'Maple has so many friends!' Lucie smiled, looking around at all the people she'd got to know in recent months.

'So do you,' he added, and she pressed her lips to his, sighing in satisfaction.

The private moment between them, in a not so private place, sent a tidal wave of love and longing through him. He pulled her against his chest, holding her tight until she squealed and laughed, and then he silenced her with more kisses. He could never get enough of kissing her, and although the twins pretended it disgusted them he could tell it didn't. They loved her nearly as much as he did.

'Get a room!' someone called.

Lucie shrugged and stuck her tongue out. Gramma May told her off, but even she was laughing.

The sun was starting to sink behind the trees. On the stage by the castle the live band began a rendition of a song he knew, and Ruby called out, 'Can we dance, Daddy?'

He turned to Lucie. There was stuff still to do... like making sure all the dogs' lights had working batteries for the great moment when they'd turn them on for the parade.

She must have read his mind. 'One dance won't hurt,' she said.

Ruby took both their hands and led them on to the dance floor. He'd never seen his daughter so happy as she'd been all this week. Having Lucie around was probably her dream come true, but he was being careful, still, not to push any parental duties on her. Everything she did must come from her own heart, and she'd already promised to help Ruby paint her bedroom.

'Come and dance with us,' she said now, pulling Josiah in with them.

The next thing Austin knew, the four of them were spinning in circles, dizzy, laughing so hard he thought he would burst.

'You call that dancing?' someone called out from the side-lines.

'Jack Granger!'

Lucie raced to get him, pushing him straight onto the dance floor in his wheelchair. Austin half expected the old grouch to complain and protest, but he let the kids push him around, a smile hovering and growing bigger and bigger by the second on his thin lips.

In the middle of the chaos, he took Lucie's hand with his good arm, beckoned her closer, and whispered something in her ear.

Lucie frowned, shook her head. 'No… No, I couldn't.'

Jack was pressing something into her hands. Lucie tried to hand it back, but Jack waved her off, then wheeled his chair back towards their event space, as if he wouldn't take no for an answer.

'What did he give you?' Austin asked, following her off the dance floor.

The twins skipped off towards Belle and Bryce.

'A necklace,' she said, stunned, holding it out to him. 'He said Alice would have wanted me to have it.'

Wow.

He swept her hair aside and fastened the sparkling necklace around her neck.

She pressed a hand to it in awe. 'It's gorgeous. Are these…real diamonds?'

'See? You do have more friends here than just Maple,' he told her, smiling away the mild disappointment that old Jack Granger had possibly outdone the gift he himself had planned.

Lucie knew she should be looking at the stars, but she couldn't tear her eyes away from AJ and the way his smile stretched his handsome face every time Ruby and Josiah got excited about a new constellation.

'That's Ursa Major,' he was saying now, whilst slipping an arm around her shoulders.

She leaned into him. The night air was warm, and it smelled like honeysuckle and all the goods from the food marquees.

While her thoughts sometimes flickered to her colleagues out in Pakistan, she didn't feel guilty any more for being here instead of there. They were happy for her, had told her how Jorge would be looking down on her, wishing her happiness. She liked to think Ebby would be wishing the same for AJ.

'Lucie, look—what's that one?'

Ruby turned the telescope towards her and she pressed her eye to the cool rim. The northern star flickered brightly, as if on cue, and she smiled, picturing Jorge's face. Weird timing...

'Make a wish,' she said to the twins.

They stared up at the sky in deep concentration, as if they couldn't decide which wish might be the most important, and AJ sneaked in a kiss to her cheek.

'I've already got my wish,' he said, nudging her.

She laughed, nudging him back.

Secretly, it turned her on. All his stupid dad jokes did, too. They reminded her that she was part of a family—one huge extended family—who wanted and needed her as much as she did them.

Maple and Jetson were stars in their own right tonight. They'd got the crowds roaring just now, doing their little tricks in their silly costumes, all lit up under the sky. Hopefully they'd raised a lot of money for Thera Pups, so they could really get AJ's venture on the map.

Now that she could help him full time, she was brimming with ideas. She and Constance were already thinking up more fundraising events. Maybe she *had* made more friends than her dog, she considered, touching a hand to the necklace.

Seeing the twins were now busy with Belle, AJ pulled her over to the merchandise stall. Most of the items were sold out already. He handed her a calendar.

'What's this?' She frowned. The Thera Pups logo and a huge photo of Jetson with his tongue out took up the front page.

'You haven't seen April yet,' he said.

His blue eyes shone with mischief and she chuckled. He looked the cutest like this, as if the young boy she'd met all those years ago had come back to play.

Intrigued, she flipped through the months. There were Samuel and Bingo, standing together with another volunteer and a basset hound. There was Jack for March, looking less than impressed while Jetson stood on his back paws by his chair. So many gorgeous photos. And then… April.

Lucy let out an excited *Eek!* at the photo of her and Maple with Constance. 'I didn't even know you'd taken that,' she said, touched.

It had been a moment in her new friend's living room, with the giant black and white photo of her happy wedding day behind them, and Maple's paw in Constance's hand. Lucie was laughing at something behind them.

'It was a pretty sweet moment,' he told her, sweeping her hair back.

She pressed a hand to her heart, kissed him. 'I shouldn't tell you this…but I like it as much as my necklace.'

'I won't tell Jack.' He grinned, glancing at the twins, still gabbling to his sister. 'I just thought… you know… You're part of this, Luce, and you always were. I hope you believe that now?'

'I do.' She smiled.

'Good—and to make sure you don't forget it, we'll put ten of these up in the living room.'

She pretended to whack him with the calendar. 'I told you… I'm not going anywhere!'

He looked serious suddenly, and she felt a nervous flutter around her heart. Until he swept her face into her hands.

'Lucie, *you* are my home.'

'And you're mine.'

All she could think was how she couldn't wait to get him back to the house and into his bedroom, where she would make love to him all night. Even if another nightmare tore her from sleep she wouldn't care. She would just roll into his arms and hold him tight.

October

'Austin, how could you do this to me on my wedding weekend?'

Belle pouted playfully at him as he entered the room, undoing two buttons on the shirt under his *Beetlejuice* jacket.

Lucie did a double-take, and a swell of pride puffed out his chest as the twins clapped their hands in glee.

'Daddy, you look so good in a stripey suit! But what's with the green hair?'

'I'll show you the movie when you're older,' he told them. 'Do what to you?' he asked Belle.

But one look at Lucie and he knew. She'd told Belle.

The wedding rehearsal was in one hour, downstairs in this sixteenth-century manor house, and Belle, in one of what was probably five or six planned outfits, pretended to cry as she flopped back onto the bed.

He hurried the twins outside and told them to count the Halloween pumpkins and paper ghosts strung up in the corridor.

'I had to tell her—look at me,' Lucie said when

they'd gone, pressing both hands to her visible bump. 'I wasn't going to, but my dress doesn't fit. We'll need the dressmaker to alter it...'

'Don't worry about that—I was only joking. We'll fix it.'

Belle jumped back to her feet, sending a glitter shower from her Tinkerbell wings all over the floor. She engulfed them both in a huge bear hug that made Maple and Jetson pad over in interest, wanting to join the excitement.

'I am so, so, *so* thrilled for you both. Lucie, when are you due?'

'April... God, I'll be huge by then.'

She fiddled with the zip on the side of a sweeping ochre-coloured V-necked gown, and Austin bit back a smile at how beautiful a pregnant Morticia Addams she made.

She was definitely bigger already. With *his* child. It had happened so quickly, once Lucie had told him that she might, possibly, if he wasn't completely opposed to the idea, quite like a baby with him.

Why wait? he'd thought.

They had the room, and plenty of money, and more than enough love to spare.

He'd gone about trying to make it happen every night and every morning—in the bath, in the car... It was almost as if the kid had been waiting there for them to say, *'We're ready to meet you...come and join our madhouse, little one.'*

'Well, luckily my crazy sister opted for a themed wedding,' he said, wrapping his arms around her, then pressing his own hands to her bump from behind.

Belle made a gagging sound, but he ignored her, kissing the side of Lucie's neck. She turned her head in its waist-length wig, dropping a kiss to his purple-stained lips.

'Dark colours mean you won't show…as much…' he said, and paused, noticing another rip along the seam of her leg. 'OK, maybe people will guess. I suppose we'll have to tell everyone else now.'

'We should tell the twins first,' she said tentatively, as Belle floated out of the room, mumbling something about them stealing her thunder.

Austin knew she was joking. She couldn't wait to dote on another niece or nephew. Since moving out, Belle had actually been back a lot more than he'd expected her to. She missed the twins, she said. Couldn't wait to have her own children with Bryce.

Austin sat Ruby and Josiah down in the Halloween-themed hall downstairs. He was nervous suddenly, holding Lucie's hand tight. They eyed him in suspicion over their orange-coloured Jack-o'-Lantern lollipops as he tried to find the words.

It was Lucie who found them first.

'Listen, you two. Your dad has something to

tell you. It's hopefully something you're going to be very, very excited about. As excited as we are!'

She crouched down to their level. An almighty rip from another busted seam made them snort with laughter.

'Oh…well, now we definitely need the dress-maker,' she laughed.

'Lucie, your dress has broken!'

'That must be the baby inside her,' Josiah said, with his toothy grin.

AJ started. Lucie stood, clutching her ripped skirt. They exchanged glances.

'We know there's a baby in your belly,' Josiah added, matter-of-factly.

'We were waiting for you to tell us,' Ruby fol-lowed up, giving Lucie a giant hug.

Her little arms only just fitted around the bump. How the…? He would never know. They were smarter than even he gave them credit for.

'Does this mean you're going to stop renewing your wedding vows every two weeks, like a cou-ple of crazy teenagers?' Belle asked, coming up behind them and thoughtfully adjusting the parrot on Ruby's pirate jacket.

Lucie grinned and looked at him sideways. It was true. Ever since their summer wedding Austin had made it a thing to regularly sweep her away somewhere for a night, so they could both renew their connection. She knew it was because he loved letting her know how much she belonged in his world, with him, and she loved him even more for it.

'Let's just enjoy your wedding weekend, shall we?' He smiled. 'The rehearsal's starting!'

He laced his fingers through Lucie's, clutched her hand tight to his side, and walked towards the aisle.

* * * * *

*If you enjoyed this story, check
out these other great reads from
Becky Wicks*

South African Escape to Heal Her
Highland Fling with Her Best Friend
The Vet's Escape to Paradise
A Princess in Naples

All available now!